THE LEGEND OF RAGNAR LOTHBROK

THE LEGEND OF RAGNAR LOTHBROK

VIKING KING AND WARRIOR

Published by Graymalkin Media
www.graymalkin.com

Copyright © 2016 by Graymalkin Media, LLC.

All rights reserved. No part of this book may be reproduced, scanned, or distributed in any printed or electronic form without permission. Please do not participate in or encourage piracy of copyrighted materials in violation of the author's rights. Purchase only authorized editions.

Picture credits:
Shutterstock: vi, 5, 103, 104, 105
iStock: 8, 71
Can Stock Photo: 5

Book design by Timothy Shaner

ISBN: 978-1-63168-063-2

Printed in the United States of America
1 3 5 7 9 10 8 6 4 2

CONTENTS

Introduction 1

The Saga of Ragnar Lothbrok 9

The Anglo-Saxon Chronicle 91

Krákumál: The Dying Ode
of Ragnar Lothbrok 105

The Tale of Ragnar's Sons 123

Gesta Danorum (Danish History) 143

INTRODUCTION

In recognition of the debut of the History Channel's fourth season of *Vikings*, this book will explore the history and the legends connected to the show's central character, Ragnar Lothbrok, along with other characters from the hit show. Included are some new translations of the medieval texts.

A Viking named Ragnar did exist and is famous for leading a Danish invasion of France in the year 845 A.D. He boldly sailed up the Seine River and marched all the way to Paris. He led thousands of Vikings; their ships were said to have clogged the river. According to the French Chronicles, the French king, Charles the Bald, was said to have divided his army with one half on each side of the river. Ragnar attacked the smaller of the two armies and easily defeated it. Then he took 111 prisoners and hung them on an island in the middle of the river where the other French division could see their bodies. It broke the spirit of the remaining division that was left to defend Paris. On Easter Sunday of 845 A.D. Ragnar sacked Paris, marched his troops in, and plundered the city. King Charles the Bald decided not to trap Ragnar inland, instead he bought peace with an offer of 7,000 pounds of silver, and Ragnar and his army were allowed to keep the plunder.

Ragnar is also widely regarded as one of the first Vikings to target Anglo-Saxon England, not just as a source of plunder, but as a future home for Danish settlers. Though Ragnar himself is not named in these early attacks by Anglo-Saxon sources, Scandinavian legends of Ragnar and his sons detail their English campaigns throughout the British Isles in the late ninth century.

There are a number of references to a Viking named Ragnar or a very similar name in various historical texts during the Middle Ages. It's debatable whether it's the same man, or if the man we know as Ragnar Lothbrok is just an amalgamation of the greatest Viking heroes of the age.

The exploits of Ragnar, or other characters from the show *Vikings*, can be found in the following medieval source texts that have been included in this volume:

The Saga of Ragnar Lothbrok is the primary source for Ragnar's legendary exploits. This thirteenth century Icelandic saga covers the origin of Ragnar's nickname, Lothbrok, his battle with a dragon, the origins of Aslaug and his marriage to her, the deeds of their sons and Aslaug in battle, and Ragnar's death at the hands of king Ella of Northumbria.

Anglo-Saxon Chronicle is the historical account of England, written year by year. Although it may be biased, taken as whole, it is the single most important historical source for English history during the early Middle Ages. While Ragnar is not specifically mentioned by name, he is largely considered to be active in the accounts of the early stages of the Viking invasions. Legend tells us that his sons, Ubbe, Ivar, and Halfdan came to England on a mission to avenge their father, who died there. The Ragnarssons are responsible for much of the devastation wrought on England during the Viking Age.

Krákumál, written in the twelfth century, is a famous poem said to be Ragnar's death song, composed and recited by Ragnar himself as he lay dying in a pit of vipers—a death sentence from an English king. Krákumál is an excellent example of Old Norse skaldic poetry.

The Tale of Ragnar's Sons is a short story written in the Middle Ages about the exploits of Ragnar's sons, mainly after Ragnar's death.

Gesta Danorum (translated as *Deeds of the Danes*) by the thirteenth-century writer Saxo Grammaticus, is an ambitious and patriotic work. After *The Saga of Ragnar Lothbrok,* Book IX of the *Gesta* provides us with the most detailed account we have about this legendary hero. Fans of the show wondering about the historical origins of Lagertha will especially enjoy this text, as Saxo explores the relationship of Ragnar and Lagertha in detail.

Ragnar Lothbrok's heroic exploits have fascinated man for over a thousand years. With so much rich, historical source material to draw from, it is no wonder that the History Channel's show *Vikings* has become so popular. As you'll see here, many of Ragnar's adventures and relationships in the show are founded in medieval source materials that recount the life of Ragnar Lothbrok and his significant legacy.

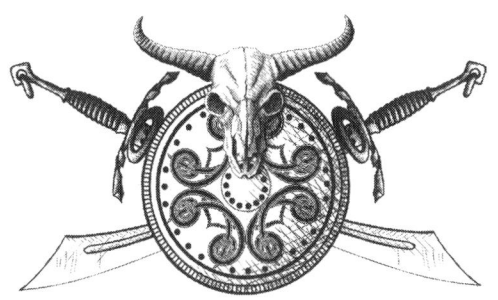

THE LEGEND OF
RAGNAR LOTHBROK

THE SAGA OF RAGNAR LOTHBROK
13TH CENTURY A.D.

Translated by Christopher Van Dyke

✢ I ✢

In Hlymdalir, Heimir heard the tidings of the death of Sigurd and Brynhild. Aslaug, their daughter and his foster child, was then three winters old. He knew that there would be an attempt to kill the girl and end her line. So great was his grief over the death of Brynhild, who had been his fosterling, and so great was his worry over Aslaug, that he no longer cared for either his kingdom or his wealth. When Heimir realized that he could not keep the girl hidden where he was, he crafted a harp that was so large that he could place Aslaug within it. Then he hid the girl inside the harp with as much gold and silver as he could carry, and he left the country. He traveled through many lands, and eventually came to the regions of the North-lands. The harp in which he carried Aslaug was so skillfully made that it could be taken apart and put together at the joints, and, whenever he could stop beside a waterfall that was nowhere near a farm, he would take the harp apart and bathe the little girl.

He had with him a *vinlauk*, which he gave to her to eat. This magical herb allowed her to grow and thrive even when they had no other food. A when the girl wept, Heimir played the harp and then she would fall silent, since Heimir was well versed in the *ithrottir* that were customary at the time. He had many glorious articles of clothes with her in the harp, and many pieces of gold. Heimir continued to travel until he arrived in Norway. He came across a small farm, which was called Spangarheith, where there was a poor man called Aki. He had a wife and she was called Grima. They were the only people living at the farm.

The day that Heimir arrived, Aki had gone into the woods and the poor woman was at home. She greeted Heimir and asked what kind of man he might be. He said he was a beggar, and asked the poor woman to give him lodgings. She said that not many came to their farm, so she could easily take him in, if he needed a place to stay. Heimir said he couldn't imagine anything more wonderful than if a fire might be lit before him, and afterward if he could be shown to the sleeping hall where he might sleep. When Grima had kindled the fire, he sat there with the harp next to him, and the poor woman was not very talkative. Often her eyes were drawn to the harp, since the fringes of one of the glorious dresses stuck out of the harp. And when he rubbed his hands before the fire, she saw one glittering gold ring showing from under his rags, since he was badly clothed. And when he had warmed himself as much as he thought was needed, then he had supper. After that, he told the poor woman to guide him to where he should sleep during the night. Grima said that it might be better for him to not stay in the main hall, "since my husband and I often talk when he comes home."

Heimir told her to do what she thought was best. Then he went out along with her. He took the harp and kept it with him. The poor woman went out until she came to a barn and said that he should stay there, and said that he might expect to enjoy his sleep there. Then Grima went on her way and busied herself with her daily tasks, and Heimir went to sleep.

When Aki came home after evening had fallen, Grima still had done little of the housework. He was weary when he came home, and very irritated with her because she had not done all the tasks she should have. The poor man said that there must be a great difference in their happiness when he worked each day past his breaking point, but she did not get on with those things that needed to be done.

"Do not be angry, husband," she said, "because it may be that you might, with just a little work, insure that we will be happy for all time."

"What is this?" asked Aki.

The poor woman answered: "A man came here to our farm, and I think that he has a lot of gold and jewels with him. He is bowed by old age, but he must have been a great hero in his day, though now he is very weary. I do not think I have seen his equal, but I think he is tired and sleepy."

The poor man said, "It seems inadvisable to me to betray one of those few who have come here."

She answered: "This is why you will forever be a little man: every task seems too large to your eyes. You have two choices—either you kill him, or I will take him as my husband, and we will drive you away. And it just so happened that you wouldn't like the way he spoke with me earlier this evening. He spoke lustfully with me, and it is my plan to take him as my husband and drive you away or kill you, if you will not do what I want."

And it is said that Aki had a domineering wife, and she continued to egg him on until he gave into her goading, took up his axe, and whetted it keenly. And when he was done, his wife led him to where Heimir slept and was then snoring greatly. Then Grima told the poor man that he should make an attack as best he could, "and then leap away quickly, since you will not be able to withstand it if he gets his hands on you." She then took the harp and went away with it.

Then the poor man went to where Heimir slept. He struck him and gave him a great wound, but he dropped his axe. At once he leaped away as quickly as he could. Heimir woke at the blow, which was his bane. And it is said that so great a din arose in his death-throes that the pillars of the house collapsed and the entire building fell down and a great earthquake occurred, and there his life ended.

Then Aki went to where Grima was, and said that he had killed him—"but for a while I was not certain how it would end, as that man was terribly powerful. But I expect that he might now be in Hell!"

The poor woman said that he should have thanks for the deed, "and I believe that now we will have plenty of money. Let us see whether or not what I suspected was true." Then they lit a fire, and the poor woman took the harp and tried to open it up, but was not able to do it any other way than breaking it, since she had no skill in the craft. And when they broke open the harp, inside it she saw a young girl of such beauty that she thought she had not seen her like before, along with many gold pieces and jewels.

Then the Aki spoke: "This is just the sort of thing that happens, that things go badly for those who betray one who trusts them. Now we have another mouth to feed."

Grima said: "This is not as I expected, but no harm will come from it." And then she asked the girl who her family might be. But the young girl did not answer, as she had not yet begun to talk.

"It has happened just as I was afraid of, that our plan turned out badly," said Aki. "We have committed a great crime. What shall we do with this child?"

"That is easy," said Grima. "We shall call her Kraka, after my mother."

Then the poor man repeated: "But what shall we do with her?" The poor woman answered: "I have a good plan: we shall call her our daughter, and raise her up."

"No one will believe that," said her husband, "as this child is much more attractive than we are. We were both born very ugly, and people will not think it likely that we would have a child like this, as uncommonly ugly as we both are."

Then the poor woman spoke: "You do not know that I have a cunning plan, so that she might not seem unlike us. I will shave her head, and rub tar and dirt on her scalp when her hair starts to grow back. We will give her a misshapen hat, and make sure she is not well clothed. We will all look alike then. Besides, it may be that men will believe that I had great beauty when I was young. Also, we will have her do all the hardest work around the farm."

Grima and Aki thought that she was unable to speak,

because as she grew up, she never answered them or spoke a word. And so it came to pass as the woman had suggested. Aslaug grew up there on the farm, and was very poor.

✢ II ✢

There was an earl called Herruth, who was mighty and famous in Gautland. He was married. His daughter was called Thora, and she was the most beautiful of all women in terms of appearance, and was most courteous in all habits and skills, which were better to have than not to have. It was her nickname that she was called Borgarhjort, since she stood out from all women in beauty as the hart does from all other animals. The earl loved his daughter very much. He had a bower made for her a short ways from his hall, and about the bower was built a wooden fence. The earl made it his custom to send his daughter a present each day for her amusement. And it is said that one day he had his daughter sent a little heather-snake, which was excessively beautiful. She was so pleased with the little snake that she kept it in an ashen box and placed gold under it for its bedding.

The snake had been there but a short while before it began to grow larger, as did the amount of gold beneath it.

It came about that eventually the snake did not have room in the ashen box, and then it lay outside of it in a ring about the box. And it afterward came about that it did not have room in the bower at all. And all the while the pile of gold grew beneath the snake precisely at the same rate. Then, when the snake lay outside around the bower, so that its head and tail could touch together, it became hard to deal with. No man dared to come to the bower on account of this snake save the one who brought it food, and the snake needed an entire ox for each meal. To the earl this seemed a terrible turn of events and he spoke this vow: that he would give his daughter to that man, whoever he might be, who killed the snake, and that pile of gold that was under the snake would be her dowry.

These tidings became known throughout the land, but nevertheless no one trusted himself to overpower the great snake.

✣ III ✣

In that time, Sigurd Hring had power over Denmark. He was a powerful king, and was famous from that great battle when he battled with Harold Hilditon at Bravella and Harold fell before him, as has become known throughout all of the northern regions. Sigurd had one son, who was called Ragnar. He was a large man, fair in appearance and with good intelligence, generous with his men but stern with his foes. Soon after Ragnar had come of age, he gathered troops and warships, and he became one of the greatest warriors, so that hardly anyone was his match. He heard what Earl Herruth had spoken regarding the great snake, but he spoke about it to no one and let on as if he did not even know about it. He then had made for himself garments in a wondrous fashion: they were shaggy-breeches and a fur-coat, and when they were done, he had them boiled in pitch. Afterward he kept them stored away.

That summer Ragnar took his war host to Gautland, and he anchored his ships in a hidden creek, which was a short distance from where the earl ruled. And when Ragnar had been there one night, he woke early in the morning, rose up and took the same shaggy-breeches and coat that were mentioned before, put on his armor, and took a great spear in his hand and went from the ship alone. And there on the beach he rolled in the sand. Before he went on his way, he took the nail holding the spear-head to the shaft out of his spear. Then he went from his ship to the earl's gate. He arrived early in the day, so that when he came all the men were still asleep. Then he turned toward the bower.

And when he came to the wooden fence where the snake was, he attacked it with his spear; he thrust the spear at it and then pulled it back, and then he attacked again. His thrust struck the snake's spine, and then he twisted the spear so that the spearhead came off the shaft; there was such a great din at the snake's death-throes that all the bower shook.

As Ragnar turned away, a jet of blood came from the snake and struck him between his shoulders, but the blood did not harm him, since the clothes that he had made protected him. And those who were in the bower woke with the din and rushed to look outside. Then Thora saw a great man going from the bower and asked him his name and whom he wanted to find. He stopped and he spoke this verse:

I have risked my famous life, beautiful woman;
  fifteen winters old
And I vanquished the earth fish.*
Near misfortune, a swift
Death for me—save
I have pierced well to the heart
The ringed salmon-of-the-heath.

And then he went on his way and did not speak more with her. And the spear-head stood in the wound afterward, but he had the shaft with him. When she had heard this verse, she understood what he had said to her about his errand and thus how old he was. And then she wondered to herself who he might be, and she thought she did not know whether he was a human being or not, since it seemed to her that he was so large for his age that he might in fact be a monster. Then she returned to the bower and went to sleep. And when men came out in the morning, they became aware that the snake was dead, and that it had been stabbed with a large spear, and the spearhead stood fast in the wound.

Then the earl had the spearhead removed, and it was so large that few could have used it as a weapon. Then the earl considered what he had said about that man who killed the snake, and he worried that he didn't know whether a human being had done this deed or not. He discussed with his friends and daughter how he should search for the hero, as it seemed likely that the man who had slain the snake would afterward seek to have the reward. His daughter advised him to have a large *moot* summoned—"and command those who do not wish to have the earl's anger and are in any way able to attend the *moot* to come here. If any there is the man who gave the snake its death wound, he shall then have the spear-shaft that goes with the spearhead."

That seemed promising to the earl, and then he had a *moot* called. And when the day came that the *moot* was to take place, the earl came and many other chieftains. Many men came from far and wide.

✣ IV ✣

It became known at Ragnar's ship that there was a *moot* to be held shortly. On the appointed day, Ragnar went from his ship with nearly all his men to the *moot*. And when they came there, they stood somewhat away from other men, since Ragnar saw that many more men had come than was customary. Then the earl stood up and asked for their silence and spoke—first he asked those men who had responded to his summons to accept his thanks; then he spoke of what had occurred; then he spoke about what he had sworn regarding the man who would kill the snake. Then finally he said, "The snake is now dead, and the man who did this famous deed left the spear standing in the wound. And if anyone who came here to the *moot* is he who has the shaft that held the spear head and that was borne away and thus may prove his claim, then I shall fulfill that which I have sworn, whoever he is, of either great or lowly rank."

And when he ended his speech, he had the spear head brought before each man who was at the *moot*, and commanded him who would claim the deed, or who had the spear-shaft that fitted the spearhead, to speak. It was so done, but none was found to be the one who had the shaft. Finally, when the spearhead came to Ragnar and was shown to him, then he acknowledged that it was his; each fitted the other, the spear-head to the shaft. Then all the men there knew that he must have killed the snake, and he became very famous in all the northern lands on account of this deed. He then asked for Thora, the earl's daughter, and the earl received this request gladly. She was given to him, and it happened that they had the largest feast with the best provisions in all the kingdom. At this feast Ragnar was married. And when the feast was over, Ragnar went to his kingdom and ruled over it and he loved Thora greatly. They had two sons: the elder was called Eirek, and the younger was called Agnar. They grew large and were handsome in appearance. They were very strong and were taller than the other men who were around. They knew all the kinds of *ithrottir*. But then it happened one day that Thora fell ill, and she died from the illness. To Ragnar this seemed so grave that he no longer desired to rule his kingdom, and he placed the kingdom in the hands of his sons and other advisors. He then took to performing his same deeds as he had before; he set out on a raiding expedition, and wherever he went he gained victory.

✢ V ✢

That summer Ragnar turned his ships to Norway, because he had many kinsmen and friends there and he wanted to visit them. One evening, he set anchor in a little harbor; there was a farm a short distance from there, which was called Spangarheith, and Ragnar and his men lay there in the harbor that night. And when morning came, the cooks went to land to bake bread. They saw that a farm was not far off, and it seemed to them that it would suit them better to go to the house and do their baking there. And when they came to this one little farm, they found someone to speak to—it was a poor woman, and they asked whether she was a housewife and what she was called. She said that she was a housewife, "and you will not lack my name. I am called Grima. But who are you?" They said that they were the liege-men of Ragnar Lothbrok, and they wanted to do their baking, "and we want you to work with us."

The poor woman answered that her hands were very stiff. "In the past I have been able to do my own work very well; but now I have myself a daughter, called Kraka, who can work with you. She will be home soon, but it has now come about that I scarcely have control over her any more." In the meantime, Kraka had gone out with the animals in the morning and had seen that many large ships had come to land, and then she went and washed herself. Grima had forbidden her to ever bathe, because she did not want men to see her beauty, because Kraka was the most beautiful of all women. Her hair was so long that it went down to the ground, and it was as fair as the most beautiful silk. Then Kraka came home. The cooks had started a fire, and Kraka saw that men had come to the farm whom she had not seen before. She looked at them and they looked at her. They asked Grima: "Is this your daughter we see, this beautiful maiden?"

"It is not a lie," said Grima. "That is my daughter you see."

"You two must be very unlike," they said, "since you are so monstrous. We have not seen a girl as beautiful, and we see that she in no way has your looks, because you are most hideous."

Grima said, "You can't see it in me now, but my appearance has changed a great deal from when I was young."

Then they agreed that Kraka would work with them. She asked: "What shall I do?" They said they wanted her to roll out the bread, and they would bake it afterward. And she then went to work, and she worked well. But the cooks all kept staring at her constantly, so they did not mind their work and the bread was burned. When they had finished the baking they went back to the ships. And there, when they brought out the meal, everyone said that they had never been given anything so terrible, and the cooks deserved to be punished for it. Then Ragnar asked why they had burned the bread. They said that they had seen a woman so beautiful that they could not focus on their work, and they thought that there was not a more beautiful woman in the entire world.

The cooks went on about her beauty so much that Ragnar cut them off, and said that he thought that there was no way that she could have greater beauty than that which Thora, his wife, had possessed. They said she was no uglier. Then Ragnar spoke: "Now I will send men there, who know how to look well. If it is thus as you have said, then your heedlessness will be forgiven of you. But if the woman is in any way uglier than you said, then you shall take a great punishment upon yourselves."

And then he sent his men to find this beautiful maiden, but the headwind was so strong that they could not leave that day, and Ragnar spoke with his messengers: "If this young maiden seems to you as beautiful as has been told, tell her to come to meet with me as I want to speak to her; I want her to be mine. I want her to be neither dressed nor undressed, neither fed nor unfed, and moreover she must not be all alone, but nevertheless no man may accompany her."

Then his men traveled until they came to the house, and they looked closely at Kraka, and it seemed to them they saw such a beautiful woman that they thought they had never before seen one as beautiful. And then they told her the words of their lord, Ragnar, and thus how she should be prepared when she went to meet with him. Kraka thought about this, how the king had spoken and how she should prepare herself. Grima thought that it could not be done, and said that she thought any king who spoke such nonsense must be a fool.

Kraka said: "He must have spoken thus because it can be done if we have the skill to discover what he was thinking." She then spoke to Ragnar's men: "However, I know that I cannot go with you today, but I will come early in the morning to your ship."

Then they went away and told Ragnar what had happened, and that she would come to the meeting. And she was at home that night. And in the early morning, Kraka told the poor man that she would go to meet with Ragnar. "But I want to alter my dress somewhat: you have a trout-net, and I want to wrap that around me, and I shall let my hair hang down over it, and I will thus be bare in no place. And I will taste of one leek—that is little food, but it will be known that I have eaten. And I will have your dog accompany me—I will thus not go all alone, even though no man accompanies me." And when Grima heard her plan, she thought that she had great cunning.

And when Kraka had made herself ready, she went on her way, until she came to the ship, and she was fair to see, as her hair was bright and looked like gold. And then Ragnar called to her and asked who she was and whom she wanted to find. She answered and spoke this verse:

I have not dared to violate your bidding,
Ragnar, when you bade me come
to your meeting, nor have I
broken the king's order.
No man is with myself,
my flesh is not clearly revealed,
I have quite fully a following,
but I come all alone.

Then he sent men to meet her, and had them accompany her to his ship. But she said she did not wish to go, unless a promise of peace might be given to her and her companion. Then she was led to the king's ship, and when she came to the foredeck he reached toward her and the dog bit him on the hand. His men leapt at it and struck the dog and tied a bow-string around its neck and it died from this—no better did those men hold with the promise of peace for her! Then Ragnar set her on the deck near himself, and spoke with her, and she answered him well and he was pleased and happy with her. He spoke this verse:

If the precious lady was merciful
to the ward of the father-land,
she might take me
to stay in her arms.

She said:

If you will honor our treaty,
king, you shall let me go
hence, spotless, to my home,
though the helmsman has pain.

✢ VI ✢

Then he said that he liked her and that he thought for certain that she should come with him. But she said it could not be thus. Then he said he wanted her to stay there for the night on the ship. She said that would not happen until he had come back from the journey he had planned,—"and it may that you will change your mind about me." Then Ragnar called for his treasurer and told him take the shirt that his wife Thora had owned and which was all embroidered with gold, and bring it to him. Then Ragnar offered it to Kraka in this manner:

> *Will you receive this shirt*
> *Which Thora Hjort had?*
> *Marked with silver, this cloth*
> *becomes you very well.*
> *Her white hands worked*
> *this garment; she was dear*
> *to the king of heroes*
> *until her death.*

Kraka spoke in reply:

> *I dare not accept the shirt*
> *Which Thora Hjort had,*
> *Marked with silver—wretched cloth*
> *is more fitting for me.*
> *I am called Kraka,*
> *for in soot-black clothes*
> *I have driven the goats*
> *along the stony paths near the waves.*

"And I will certainly not take this shirt," she said. "I will not be arrayed in fine clothes while I am with this poor couple. It may be that you would consider me fairer if I were adorned more fairly, but I will now go home. And when you return, you may send men to find me me, if the matter is still the same in your mind and you still want me to go with you." Ragnar said that he would not change his mind, and she went home.

And so Ragnar and his men went as they had intended as soon as they had wind, and he set about his errand to Norway as he had planned. And when he was returning home, he came to the same harbor as he had before when Kraka had come to him. And that same evening he sent men to find her and speak Ragnar's words—that she should prepare to depart for good. But she said that she could not leave before the morning. Kraka rose up early and went to the bed of the poor man and woman and asked whether they were awake. They said they were awake and asked what she wanted. She said that she wished to leave and be there no longer.

"And I know that you killed Heimir, my foster-father, and I have no one to reward with more ill than you. But I have been with you a long time, and for this reason I will not let evil be done to you. However, I will now declare that each day will be worse for you than the one that came before it, but the last will be the worst of all—and now I will depart." Then she went and proceeded to the ship, and there she was well received. They were given good weather. Then that same evening, when men prepared their beds,

Ragnar said that he wanted Kraka and him to sleep together. She said it could not be thus, "for I want you to drink a wedding feast for me, when you come to your kingdom; that seems more fitting to my honor and to you and our offspring, if we have any."

He granted her request, and the rest of their journey went well. Ragnar then came home to his land, and a glorious feast was prepared for his return; then there was joyful drinking for both his return and his wedding. And the first evening, when they came together in one bed, Ragnar wished to consummate their marriage, but she asked to avoid that, because she said that some evil might afterward be born out of it if her advice was ignored. Ragnar said that could not be true, and he said that the poor man and women were not prophetic, if they were the ones who had put this in her mind. He asked how long she would make him wait. Then she said:

Three nights shall thus pass,
apart in the evening, although
settled together in one hall,
before our sacrifice to the holy gods;
thus shall this denial
prevent a lasting harm to my son—
he whom you are hasty to beget
will have no bones.

And although she said that, Ragnar gave it no heed, and followed his own advice.

✣ VII ✣

A little while passed, and their marriage was good, and full of love. Then Kraka knew herself to be pregnant, and it progressed until she gave birth to a boy, and he was sprinkled with water and given a name and called Ivar. The boy was born without bones and there was cartilage where his bones should have been. Still, when he was young, he grew so strong that none was his match. He was of all men most handsome in appearance and so wise that none was known who was a wiser councilor than he. It happened that more children were granted them. Another son they called Bjorn, the third Hvitserk, the fourth Rognvald. They were all great men, very valiant, and as soon as they could learn them, they became well versed in all the *ithrottir*. And wherever they went, Ivar had himself borne on staves, as he could not walk, and he advised his brothers in whatever they did.

Eirek and Agnar, Ragnar's sons from Thora, were such great men themselves that their like could hardly be found, and they went in their war-ships every summer and were renowned for their harrying. And then it happened one day that Ívar asked his brothers, Hvitserk and Bjorn, how long might pass by while they sat at home rather than having their renown increased as well. And they said that they would act on his advice in that as in all other things.

Ivar said, "Now I want us to ask to have ships prepared for us, and troops enough to man them, and then I want us to gain gold and glory for ourselves, if it is possible." And when they had decided upon that plan among themselves, they told Ragnar that they wanted him to get them ships and veteran troops who were experienced in the seizing of treasure, and well prepared for anything. And he gave this to them as they asked. And then, when their troops were prepared, they traveled from that land. And wherever they fought with men, they got the best of them and earned for themselves both many troops and much treasure. And then Ivar said that he wanted them to continue on until a more powerful force was before them, and thus they might test their prowess. And then they asked where he knew to find such a force. And then he named a place, which was called Hvitabaer, where pagan sacrifices were held—"and many have sought to conquer that place, but none have not been victorious." Ragnar himself had come there but had to fall back without having achieved his goal.

"Are the forces there so great," they asked, "and so hardy, or are there other difficulties?" Ivar said both that the thronging troops were great and the place of sacrifice was powerful, so all that had gone against it had not been victorious. And then they said that he should advise whether they should set a course for there or not. And he said that he desired greatly to discover what might be the greater: their own hardiness, or the magical powers of the people there.

✢ VIII ✢

So the brothers set a course for Hvitabaer, and when they came to that land they prepared to disembark. And they thought it necessary that some of the troops keep guard over the ships. And Rognvald, their brother, was so young that they thought him to be unready for such great perils as they would likely face, and so they had him guard the ships with some of the troops. And after they went from the ships, Ivar said that the garrison had two cows, young geldings, and men turned and fled before these cattle, as they could not stand their bellowing and their troll-like form. Then Ivar said: "Bear yourselves as best you can, although you feel some fear, because nothing will harm you." Then they departed with their troops. And when they drew near the fortress, it happened that they who lived in that place became aware of them, and they loosed the cattle that they had great faith in. And when the geldings were let loose, they leaped forward fiercely and roared terribly. Then Ivar saw them from where he was borne upon a shield, and he told his men to bring his bow, and it was done. Then he shot at the evil geldings, so that they both received their deaths, and then the battle that the men had most feared was ended. Then Rognvald began to speak back at the ships, and he said to the troops that those men were fortunate who should have such entertainment as his brothers had. "And there is no other reason that I should remain behind except that they wished to have all the glory. But now we shall all go ashore."

And then they did so. And when they came upon the troops, Rognvald went fiercely into the fray, and it happened thus that he fell in battle and was slain. Then the brothers came to the fortress, and they took to the fray anew. It happened then that the men of the fortress took to flight, and the brothers pursued the fleeing host. And when they returned afterward to the fortress, Bjorn spoke this verse:

We fell with a cry
upon Gnifafirth, our swords
biting fiercer than theirs,
I may truly say.
Each who wished to could become
a killer of men out before Hvitabaer;

*let young men
spare not their swords!*

Then when they came back to the fort, they took all the treasure and burned the houses within the fortress, and broke down all the battlements. And then they sailed their ships thence.

✠ IX ✠

There was at that time a king called Eystein who ruled over Svithjoth. He was married and had one daughter. She was called Ingibjorg. She was the prettiest of all women and beautiful to behold. King Eystein was powerful and had many followers. He was ill-tempered, though wise. He had settled himself at Uppsala. He was a great sponsor of sacrifices, and there were so many sacrifices at Uppsala at that time that nowhere in the Northlands held more. The king and his people had great faith in one cow, and they called her Sibilja. She had been offered so many sacrifices that men could not stand before her bellowing, so powerful had her magic become. The king was wont, when an overwhelming army was expected, to send this cow in front of his host; such great devilish power filled her that all his foes became so maddened as soon as they heard her that they fought among themselves and cared not for their own safety. Because of this, Svithjoth was unharried by assaults, for men dared not contend against such power. King Eystein had friendship with many men and chieftains, and it is said that at that time there was a great friendship between the Kings Eystein and Ragnar, and this was their custom—that they should, alternating each summer, prepare a feast for the other. Then it came about that Ragnar was to go to a feast of King Eystein's. And when he came to Uppsala, there was a good welcome for him and his men. And when they drank together on the first evening, the king had his daughter fill the cups for himself and Ragnar. And Ragnar's men said among themselves that Ragnar would surely ask for King Eystein's daughter if only he was not married to the poor couple's daughter. And then it happened that one of his men brought this to his attention; and thus in the end it happened that the princess was promised to Ragnar as his bride, but she would stay merely as his betrothed for a some time.

And then when their feast was ended, Ragnar journeyed homeward, and it went well for him—but nothing is said of his journey before he came a short distance from his fortress, and his path lay through a wood. When they came to a clearing in the forest, Ragnar brought his troops to a halt and asked for their silence and told all his men, who had been with him on his journey to Svithjoth, that they should say nothing of his intent to enter into marriage with King Eystein's daughter. Then he laid so strict a penalty on this that whosoever spoke of it would receive nothing less than the loss of his life. And when he had spoken what he had wanted, he went home. And then it happened that men rejoiced when he came back, and there was drinking and a joyous banquet in his honor.

And then he came to his high seat. He had not been sitting there long when Kraka came into the hall before Ragnar and sat on his knee and laid her arms about his neck and asked: "What are your tidings?" But he said he knew of nothing to tell her. And when the evening came, men took to drinking, and afterward they went to sleep. And when Ragnar and Kraka came into the same bed, she asked him yet again for tidings, and he said he did not know any. Then she wished to converse more, but he said he was very sleepy and weary from traveling.

"Now I can tell you tidings," she said, "if you will not tell any to me."

He asked what they might be.

"I call it great tidings," she said, "when a woman is promised to a king, although some men say that he already has a wife."

"Who told you this?" asked Ragnar.

"Your men will keep their lives and limbs, since none of those men told this to me," she said. "You remember how three birds sat in a tree near you? They told me these tidings. I ask this of you—that you not stay fixed on this course of action as you intend. Now I shall tell you that I am the daughter of a king and not of that poor couple, and my father was such a great man that none have proved themselves his equal, and my mother was the most beautiful of all women and the wisest. Her name shall be lifted up as long as the world is standing."

Then he asked who her father was, if she was not the daughter of the poor man who was living at Spangarheith. She said that she was the daughter of Sigurd Fafnir's Bane and Brynhild Buthladottur.

"It seems to me very unlikely that their daughter would be called Kraka and their child might wind up in such poverty as there was at Spangarheith."

She answered thus: "This is the story," and then she spoke and brought forth the tale of Sigurd and Brynhild meeting on the mountain and how she was begotten. "And when Brynhild gave birth, a name was given me, and I was called Aslaug." And then she spoke of everything that had happened until she met the poor man.

Then Ragnar answered: "I am surprised by these mad-ramblings about Aslaug which you speak."

She answered: "You know that I am with child. It will be a male child that I have, and this mark will be on the boy: that it will seem that a snake lies within the boy's eyes. And if this comes about, I ask this—that you do not go to Svithjoth at the time that you would receive the daughter of King Eystein. But if this fails to come about, go if you want. But I want the boy to be called after my father if in his eyes is that mark of glory, as I think there will be."

Then it came to the time when she knew herself to be in labor, and she delivered a boy. Then the serving women took the boy and sprinkled him with water. Then she said that they should bear him to Ragnar and let him see him. And then this was done, and thus the young man was borne unto the hall and laid in the lap of Ragnar's cloak. And when he saw the boy, he was asked what he should be called. He spoke a verse:

Sigurd will the boy be called—
he will thus conduct himself in battle
much like the father of his mother,
after whom he is called.
Thus will the greatest of
Odin's race be named,
the snake-eyed one,
and he will bring much death!

Then he pulled a ring from off his hand and gave it to the boy as a *nafnfestr*. But as he reached forth his hand with the gold, the baby turned so that the ring touched the back of the boy, and Ragnar deemed that to mean that he would hate gold. And then he spoke a verse:

He will be pleasing to heroes,
the dear son of Brunhild's daughter,
who has gleaming brow-stones
 and a most faithful heart.
Thus the sword's messenger
bears himself better than all Vikings;
Buthli's descendent, who quickly
disdains the red rings.

And again he spoke:

I have never seen
bridles in the brow-stones
of the beard-slopes of the brow,
save in Sigurd alone.
This vigorous beast chaser
has taken mirkwood-rings
into the field of his eyelids—
thus by this sign is he known.

Then Ragnar said that they should bear the boy out to the bower. And that was the end of his going to Svithjoth. And then the family-line of Aslaug came out, and every man knew that she was the daughter of Sigurd Fafnir's Bane and Brynhild Buthladottur.

✣ X ✣

When the time had passed when it had been agreed that Ragnar would go to his wedding at Uppsala and he had not come, it seemed to King Eystein that this brought dishonor upon himself and his daughter; and then the friendship between the kings was ended. And when Eirek and Agnar, Ragnar's sons, heard that, they then plotted between themselves to go with as many troops as they might muster, that they might harry in Svithjoth. And then they gathered together many troops and readied their ships, and it seemed to them very important that all went well when the ships set forth. Then it happened that Agnar's ship slipped off the launch rollers, and a man was in the way and was killed: and they called that "the reddening of the rollers." This seemed to them not to be a good beginning, but they would not let that stand in the way of their journey. And when their troops were prepared, they traveled with their troops to Svithjoth, and there, when they came quickly to King Eystein's kingdom, they traveled across it with war-shields.

But the men of that land became aware of them and went to Uppsala and told King Eystein that they had come to the land. And the king had a message sent in the form of an arrow throughout his kingdom and thus gathered so many men together that it was wondrous. And then he traveled with them until he came to a forest, and they there set up their camp. He then had with him the cow Sibilja, and many were the sacrifices to her before she would travel.

And when they were in the forest, King Eystein spoke:

"I have news," he said, "that Ragnar's sons are on the field beside this forest, and it was said to me truly that they do not have a third of our troops. Now we shall arrange our host for battle, and a third of our troops shall go to meet them first, and they are so unflinching that they will think they have us in their power. Immediately afterward we shall come at them with all our might, and our cow shall go before our troops, and it seems to me that they will not hold before her bellowing."

And then it was so done. And as soon as the brothers saw King Eystein's troops they thought that their foes did not have power greater than theirs, and it did not occur to them that there might be more troops. And soon after all the troops came from the forest and the cow was set loose, and she leaped before the troops and went about fiercely. So great a din arose that the warriors who heard it fought among themselves, except for the two brothers holding their ground. The evil creature struck many a man with her horns that day, and Ragnar's sons, though they were powerful in themselves, thought they might not stand against both the great crowd and the pagan sacrificial-magic. However, they faced it unflinchingly and guarded themselves well and bravely and with great renown. Eirek and Agnar, were at the front of the host that day, and often they went against the host of King Eystein.

But then Agnar fell. Eirek saw that and then bore himself most boldly and did not care whether he came away or not. Then he was overborne by the great force and seized. And then Eystein declared that the battle should stop, and offered Eirek peace. "And I will lay this offer before you," he said, "that I will give you my daughter." Eirek replied, and spoke this verse:

> *I will not hear an offer for my brother,*
> *nor buy the maid with rings*
> *from Eystein, who spoke the words*
> *of Agnar's death.*
> *My mother will not weep;*

*set me up to stand
pierced through by a forest of spears—
at the last, I choose to die.*

Then he said that he wanted the men who had followed them to have peace to go wherever they wished. "And I wish to have as many spears as possible taken up, then have the spears set up in the ground, and I wish myself to be lifted up upon them—there I want to leave life." Then King Eystein said that that would be done thus, as he asked, though he chose that which went worse for them both. Then the spears were set up, and Eirek spoke a verse:

*I think that no king's son
shall die on so dear a bed:
a day-meal to ravens,
as I know my fate to be.
The livid blood-flies
shall break both brother's bodies
and soon shriek over us,
though that be a bad reward.*

And then he went to where the spears were set up and he took a ring off his hand and cast it to those who had followed him and who had been given peace, and he commended it to Aslaug and spoke a verse:

Bear you my last words,
you east-faring troops,
that the slender maid, Aslaug
is to have my rings.
Then to the greatest of mothers,
my mild stepmother, you may
speak of me, her son,
and of my glorious spear-death.

And then he was heaved up on the spears. Then he saw where the raven flew, and again he spoke:

The sea-mew rejoices over the head
of my now wounded corpse;
the wound-hawk craves
my unseeing eyes.
I think if the raven
strikes out my eyes,
the wound-hawk ill rewards the many times
Ekkil has given him his fill.

Then he gave up his life with great valor. And his messengers went home and did not let up until they came to where Ragnar had residence. And then Ragnar's sons had not come home from raiding. They were there for three nights before they went to meet with Aslaug. And when they came before Aslaug in her high-seat, they greeted her worthily; she received their greeting. She had one linen handkerchief upon her knee, and she had unloosed her hair, and she intended to comb it. Then she asked who they were, since she had not seen them before. He who spoke on their behalf said that they had been among the troops of Eirek and Agnar, the sons of Ragnar. Then she spoke a verse:

> *What is said by you,*
> *friends of the king, what news?*
> *Are the Swedes still in their land,*
> *or otherwise driven out?*
> *I have heard that the*
> *Danes went from the south;*
> *the chiefs had bloody rollers.*
> *But since then, I know nothing.*

He spoke a verse in reply:

> *There is need, woman,*
> *that we tell you*
> *that Thora's sons are dead;*
> *cruel are the fates to your man!*
> *I know no other tale as heavy as this;*
> *now we have come from*

hearing the news: the eagle flies
over the corpse of the dead man.

Then she asked how that had happened. And then he spoke the verse, which Eirek had spoken, when he had sent her the ring. They say that she then let a tear fall, and it had the appearance of blood, but it was as hard as a hailstone. No man had seen that—that she had let fall a tear—either before or after. Then she said that she might not pursue vengeance before they came back home: that is, Ragnar or his sons. "And you shall be here until then; I shall not hold off spurring on vengeance as if they had been my own sons." Then they stayed there.

And it so happened that Ivar and the brothers came home before Ragnar, and they were not home long before Aslaug went to find her sons. Sigurd was then three winters old. He went with his mother. And then when she came into the hall, where the brothers were discussing, they received her well. Each asked the other for tidings, and they spoke first of the fall of Rognvald, her son, and of the circumstances, and how it had happened. But that did not seem grave to her, and she said:

My sons leave me by myself
to gaze over the sea-mews;
you do not travel from

house to house, begging.
Rognvald took up the shield,
red with men's blood;
youngest of all my sons
he came to Odin.

"And I cannot see," she said, "that he could have lived to a greater honor." Then they asked her what tidings she had. She answered: "The fall of Eirek and Agnar, your brothers, my stepsons. I think, that out of all men, they had the best courage. And it will not be odd if you do not bear such an injury, but take great vengeance. I will be of great assistance to you in all of this, so that this deed should be more than commonly avenged."

Then Ivar said, "This is true—I will never come to Svithjoth eagerly to battle with King Eystein and the pagan sacrificial-magic which is there." She pressed him greatly, but Ivar spoke for all of them, and he refused outright to make the journey. And then she spoke this verse:

You would not be
unavenged by your brothers
one season later
if you had died first;
I would prefer

that Eirek and Agnar
had lived in your stead,
though as sons they were not born to me.

"It is not certain," Ivar said, "whether the matter will stand differently, even if you speak one verse after another. However, do you know clearly what strongholds there are before us?"

"I do not know for certain." she said. "However, what can you say of the difficulties there might be?"

Ivar said that there was very great pagan sacrificial magic, and he said that no man has ever heard of it's like. "And the king is both powerful and ill-natured."

"What does he have the most faith in when making sacrifices?"

He said: "That is a great cow, and she is called Sibilja. She is so great in might that as soon as men hear her bellowing his foes are unable to stand, it is scarcely as if the battle is fought with men at all. It rather seems that they must face beings of troll-like form before they face the king, and I will risk neither myself or my troops there."

She said: "One might think that you cannot both be called a great man and not strive to be one."

And when it then seemed to her that matters were beyond hope, she decided to leave, she thought they did not value her words. Then Sigurd Worm-in-Eye spoke: "I will tell you, Mother," he said, "how it seems to me, though I might not affect their answers."

"I wish to hear that," she said. Then he spoke a verse:

If you grieve, mother,
the household shall become
ready in three nights;
the road we have is long.
King Eystein shall not
rule in Uppsala
even if he offers us treasure,
if you aid and push us on.

And when he had spoken that verse, the brothers rethought their plans somewhat. And then Aslaug said: "You now declare rightly, my son, that you shall do my will. And yet I cannot see how we might make this to come to pass if we do not have your brothers' assistance. It may happen as it seems best to me—that this vengeance of yours will come about—and it seems to me that you proceed rightly my son." And then Bjorn spoke a verse:

Though little is said in speech,

a man may turn over
vengeance in his heart,

in his hawk-swift chest.
We do not have a serpent
nor a shining snake in our eyes,
but my brothers gladdened me:
I will remember your stepsons.

And then Hvitserk spoke a verse:

Let Agnar's bane
now rejoice little;
but we must think before
we say that there might be vengeance.
We must push out a ship onto the waves,
Break up the ice before the stern;
We must see which
ships might be swiftly prepared.

And Hvitserk spoke of this, that the ice must be broken, for the frost was then great, and their ships were in ice. And then Ivar began to speak and said that it had come to the point when he must take some part in it, and then he spoke a verse:

You have both honor and
courage in this vengeance,
but you might lack this—

a strong, obstinate following.
You shall bear me
before the heroes;
I will take the path to vengeance,
though I may use neither boneless hand.

"And now," said Ivar, "we must devise the best plans we may for gathering warships and warriors, as we must not spare in this if we are to conquer." Then Aslaug went away.

✷ XI ✷

Sigurd had a foster-father, and he gathered for his foster-son both ships and troops that were well prepared. This was done so quickly that the troops that Sigurd was to have prepared were readied when three nights had passed; he also had five ships, all well prepared. And then when five nights had passed, Hvitserk and Bjorn had prepared fourteen ships. When seven nights were passed from that time when they had conceived and declared their voyage, Ivar had ten ships and Aslaug another ten. Then they all spoke together, and told each other how many troops they had gathered. And then Ivar said that he would sent mounted troops by land.

Aslaug said: "If I had known for certain that troops that went by land might have been useful, I might have sent some troops as well."

"We shall not delay for that," said Ivar. "We shall now go with those troops that we have gathered together."

Then Aslaug said that she would go with them, "for I know best what pains must be taken to bring about vengeance for these brothers."

"This is certain," said Ivar, "that you will not come in our ships. If you so desire, you may command the troops that go by land." She said it would be thus. Then her name was changed, and she was called Randalin.

Then the troops both left, but before they did, Ivar told them where they should meet. Then both parties fared well, and they met as they had planned. And when they had thus come to Svithjoth and the kingdom of King Eystein, they traveled across the land with war-shields. Thus they burned all that was before them, killed every man's son, and moreover killed all those who were living.

✢ XII ✢

It happened that that some men escaped and found King Eystein and told him that to his kingdom had come an army that was powerful and thus difficult to deal with, and that would not leave anything unharmed. They had pillaged all that they had come across so that no house was still standing. When King Eystein heard these tidings, he thought he knew who these Vikings might be. And then he had a summons sent by arrow throughout his entire kingdom, and he summoned all those who were his men and who wished to give him troops and might bear shields.

"We shall have with us our cow Sibilja, who is a god, and let her leap before the troops. It seems to me that it will go as before, that they will not be able to stand before her bellowing. I will encourage all my troops to do their best, and thus drive off the large and evil force."

And then it was thus done, that Sibilja was let loose. And then Ivar saw her charge and heard the hideous bellowing that was coming out of her. He thought that all the troops should make a great noise, both with weapons and war-cry, so that they would barely hear the voice of that evil creature when she charged toward them. Ivar spoke with his carriers, telling them that they should bear him forward so that he might be closer to the front.

"And when you see the cow come at us, cast me at her, and it shall go one way or the other—that I shall lose my life, or she shall have her bane. Now you must take one mighty elm tree and carve it into the shape of a bow, along with arrows." And when this strong bow was brought to him along with the great arrows that they had made, they did not think that any man could actually wield them. Then Ivar encouraged his men to do their best. Then the troops went with great vigour and making much noise, and Ivar was borne before their battle array.

Such a great din arose when Sibilja bellowed that they heard it just as well as if they had been silent and standing still. Then that caused it to happen that the troops fought among themselves, all save the brothers. And when this wonder took place, those who bore Ivar saw that he drew his bow as if he held a weak elm branch, and it seemed as if he drew the arrow point back past his bow. Then they heard a louder twang from his bow than they had ever heard before. And then they saw that his arrows flew as swift as if he had shot a strong crossbow and they saw it happen that the arrows came to sit in each of Sibilja's eyes. And then she fell, but after that she went on headfirst, and her bellowings were much worse than before.

And when she came at them, he commanded them to cast him at her, and he became to them as light as if they cast a little child, because they were not very near the cow when they cast him and yet he flew like a stone from a sling. And then he came down heavily upon the cow Sibilja, and he became then as heavy as a boulder when he fell on her, and every bone in her was broken, and she received her death. Then he commanded his men to take him up again quickly. And then he was taken up, and his voice was ringing so that all heard when he spoke, and it seemed to all the army as if he was standing near each man, though he was far off. It became perfectly silent as he gave his orders. And he spoke to this end—that the warring, which they had come for, was soon to be all finished, and no harm was done when the troops had skirmished briefly among themselves.

Then Ivar encouraged them to wreak great harm upon those they had fought. "And now it seems to me that the most violent of them is gone, since the cow is slain." And then both armies had their troops drawn up, and together they clashed in battle, and the battle was so difficult that all the Swedes said that they never had had such a trial of their manhood. And then both brothers, Hvitserk and Bjorn, went at them so hard that no battle-array could stand against them. And then so many of King Eystein's troops fell that a scant few remained standing, and some decided to flee.

And their battle concluded thus—that King Eystein fell, and the brothers had the victory. And then they gave quarter to those that lived after the battle. And then Ivar said that he did not wish to harry in that land, because that land was now lacking a leader. "And I would that we hold course until a greater opposition is before us." But Randalin journeyed home with some troops.

✢ XIII ✢

Then they decided among themselves that they should harry in the Southern Kingdom. And Sigurd Worm-in-Eye, Randalin's son, went with his brothers on every raid after that. In these raids they strove against every town that was strong, and they fought so that none could prevail against them.

And then they heard that there was one town that was both strong and full of hardy men. And then Ivar said that he wanted to head for it. And this is said of what the town was called and who ruled over it: the chieftain was called Vifil, and his namesake was a town called Vifilsborg. Then they traveled with war-shields so that they desolated all the towns that they happened upon, until they came to Vífilsborg. The chief was not at home in his town, and many of his troops were away with him. Then they set up their tents on the plains that were about the town. They were peaceful during the day when they came to the town, and they held a talk with the townsmen. Ragnar's sons asked the townsmen whether they would rather give up the town, and in return they would all be granted peace, or rather test their forces and their hardihood, and their men would then receive no quarter.

But they responded quickly and said that the town would never be so overcome. "But before that happens, you must try us and show us your valor and zeal." Then the night passed. And the very next day they went to strive against the town but could not overcome it. They sat around the town for half a moon and they strove every day with different strategies, that they might get the town.

But it happened that they were no nearer victory after a long while, and they then decided to turn away from there. And when the townsmen became aware that they were planning to turn away from there, then they went out to the town walls and spread out their valuables and they draped all those clothes that were the finest in the town over the city walls, and they laid out their gold and their valuables. And then one of their troop took to words and spoke: "We thought that these men, the sons of Ragnar, and their troops were hardy men, but we can see that they have not come nearer to victory than others." Then after that they shouted at them and beat upon their shields and egged them on the best they could. And when Ivar heard that, he was so greatly startled that he fell into a great sickness, so that he might not stir, and they had to wait until it came about that he either recovered or he died. He lay there all that day until evening, and spoke not a word. And then he spoke with those men who were with him, saying that they should tell Bjorn, Hvitserk, and Sigurd and all the wisest men that he wanted to hold a talk with them.

And when they all came and were in one place, those who were the greatest leaders among the troops, then Ivar asked if they had devised any tactic that was likely to succeed more than those that they had tried before. But they all answered that they did not have such wit in these matters that they might devise a tactic which would be successful. "Now, as often, you are the one whose advice might be useful."

Ivar answered thus: "One plan has come to me in my mind, which we have not tried. There is a large forest not far from here, and now, when night falls, we shall travel from our tents secretly to the forest, but we will leave our war-tents standing here, and when we come to the forest, each man shall bind branches for himself. And when that is done, we shall attack the town from all sides and strike fire in the wood, and there will then be a great blaze, and the town walls will then lose their lime because of the fire. And we shall then bring up our war-slings and see how hardy they are."

And thus it was done: they traveled to the forest, and they were there as long as Ivar deemed necessary. Then they attacked to the town in accordance with his arrangements, and then when they had struck fire in the large pile of wood there was so great a blaze that the walls could not stand it and they lost their lime. Then Ivar's troops brought their war-slings up to the town and broke a large gap in the walls, and a battle began. And as soon as the two forces stood evenly opposed in battle, then the troops of townsmen fell, and some fled before them, and some, in the end, fled to their ships. They killed every man's child who was in the town, and they took all the goods and burnt the town before they went on their way.

✣ XIV ✣

Then they set out from there until they came to the town called Lúna. By then they had broken nearly every town and every castle in all the Southern Kingdom, and they were then so famous in all that region that there was no child, however young, that did not know their name. Then they planned not to let up until they had come to Rome, because that town was then both very mighty and full of men, and famous and rich. But they did not quite know how long a distance it was to that town, and they had such a large troop that they could not supply provisions for them.

And when they were at the town of Luna they discussed the journey among themselves. Then there came a man, who was old and cunning. They asked what sort of man he was, and he said that he was a poor beggar and had, for all his life, journeyed across the land.

"You must then know many things you can tell us, which we want to know."

The old man answered: "I do not know of anything that I will be unable to tell you, whatever land you want to ask of."

"We want you to tell us how far it is to Rome from here."

He answered: "I can show you something to indicate that. You may see here these ancient iron shoes, which I have on my feet, and these others, which I carry on my back, which are now worn out. But when I set out from there, I bound these worn-out ones on my feet, which I now have on my back, and at that time both sets were new. I have been on the road ever since."

And when the old man had said that, they thought that they could not continue on the way to Rome, as they had intended among themselves. And then they turned away with their warriors and captured many towns that had never been captured before, and proof of this can be seen to this day.

✣ XV ✣

Now the story goes that Ragnar was sitting at home in his kingdom and he did not know where his sons were, or Randalin, his wife. But he heard tales from all his men that none might be equal to his sons, and it seemed to him that none were as famous as they.

Then he wondered how he might gain fame that would not be any less long lived. He thought about this to himself, and then he sent for his craftsmen and had them fell wood for two large cargo ships, and men heard that these two vessels were so large that such ships had never been made in the North-lands. Then he gathered from all his kingdom a large mass of arms, and from these actions men discerned that he had decided on some war-expedition in foreign lands. This news became known in all the neighboring lands, and so all the men who lived in those lands, and the kings who ruled them, feared that they might not be able to remain in their kingdoms. And they all had watches set up on their borders, in case Ragnar might attack them.

One day Randalin asked Ragnar where he was intending on harrying. He told her that he intended to go to England with only the two large ships which he had built, and as many troops as they might carry. Then Randalin said: "This journey that you are planning seems very imprudent to me. I have a mind to advise you to have more boats, but smaller, more war-like ones."

"There is no glory," he said, "if men conquer a land with many ships. But there is no tale of any who have conquered such a land as England with only two ships. And if I do suffer defeat, it will be better if I have taken just a few ships from this land."

Then Randalin answered: "It seems to me no less expensive to build these two massive ships than to have built more long-ships for this journey. You know that it is difficult for ships to make the crossing to England. If it happens that your ships sink, then even if your men manage to make it to land they will then be slain if the lord of the land comes across them. It is better to invade their harbors in long-ships than in merchant vessels!"

Then Ragnar spoke this verse:

No bold man may spare the
amber of the Rhine if he desire warriors;
but many rings help a wise chieftain
worse than war-like men.
It is bad to defend
the town-gates with red-gold rings;
I know very many dead boars
whose treasure yet lives on.

Then he had his ships readied and his men gathered, so that the merchant vessels were fully loaded. There was much discussion about his plans. But he spoke this one verse:

What is it that I, the breaker of rings,
hear roaring from the rocks:
that the distributor of the fire of the hand
should abandon the difficult serpents of the sea?
I, the scatterer of the
forearm bands, shall, bejeweled goddess,
follow my plan, unwavering,
if the gods are willing.

And when his ships and those troops that would accompany him were ready, and when it seemed as if good weather would come, Ragnar said that he would go to the ships. And when he was ready, Randalin accompanied him to the ships. But before they parted, she said that she would reward him for that shirt that he had given her. He asked what manner of reward it would be, and she spoke a verse:

I sewed for you
a shirt with no seams;
with hale heart I wove it
out of the gray wool;
wounds will not bleed,
nor will edges bite
through this invincible shroud
which is blessed by the gods.

He said that he would accept this aid. And then when they parted, it was evident that their parting seemed very difficult for her.

Then Ragnar held course in his ships to England, as he had planned. He received a bitter wind, so that he broke both his merchant vessels against the rocky coast of England, but all his troops managed to come to shore without losing their clothes or weapons. Once ashore, whenever he came to farms or towns or castles, he conquered them.

There was a king called Ella, who at that time ruled England. He heard the rumours when Ragnar first left his own land, and so he sent forth men to watch the seas, so that he might know as soon as Ragnar came to land. Now these men journeyed to meet with King Ella, and told him tidings of war. Then he had a summons sent throughout all his land and commanded every man come to him who could wield a shield and ride a horse and who dared to fight. He gathered so many together there that it was a wondrous thing.

Then King Ella and his men prepared for battle. He spoke to his troops: "If we gain victory in this battle, and it happens that you know that it is Ragnar who has come against us, then you must be sure not to slay him, because he has sons who would never again leave us in peace if he fell."

At the same time, Ragnar was preparing for battle, and he wore that shirt that Randalin had given him at their parting over his mail, and in his hand was that spear with which he had vanquished the snake that lay about Thora's bower and which no one else had dared to face, and he had no other protection save his helm.

And when the two armies met, the battle began. Ragnar had many fewer troops. The battle had not been going long before most of Ragnar's troops fell. But wherever he went that day, the army cleared away before him. He struck at their shields or mail or helms, and so great were his blows that none could stand before them. It happened with all who shot or hewed at him that not one weapon did him any harm, and he never received a wound—but he killed a great multitude of King Ella's troops. However, the battle ended so that all of Ragnar's troops fell, and he was overborne with shields and seized.

Then he was asked who he was, but he was silent and did not answer. Then King Ella spoke: "We will put this man to a great trial if he will not tell us who he is. He shall be cast into a snake pit, and let him sit there a very long while. But if he says anything by which we might know he is Ragnar, then he shall be taken out as quickly as possible."

Then Ragnar was led from there and he sat in the pit a very long while, but no snakes fastened onto him. Then the men said: "This man is very strong: he was not bitten by a weapon all day, and now no snakes harm him." Then King Ella said that he was to be stripped of the outermost clothing that he had on; thus it was done, and all the snakes hung on him on all sides. Then Ragnar said: "The young pigs would now squeal if they knew what the older one suffered." And though he spoke thus, they did not know for certain that it was Ragnar who was held rather than another king. Then he spoke a verse:

> *I have had fifty*
> *and one battles*
> *which were thought glorious:*
> *I made much harm.*
> *I did not look to*
> *a snake to be my bane;*
> *things happen very often to one*
> *that one thinks of the least.*

And he spoke another:

> *The young pigs would squeal*
> *if they knew the state of the boar;*
> *of the injury done to me.*
> *Snakes dig in my flesh,*
> *stab at me harshly,*

and have sucked on me;
soon now will my body
die among the beasts.

Then he gave up his life, and he was taken out of pit. And King Ella thought he knew that it was Ragnar who had given up his life. He wondered to himself how he might know for certain, and how he could protect his kingdom and how he could learn the Ragnarssons' reaction when they learned of their father's death. He decided on a plan: he then readied a ship and chose a man to carry out that plan, who was both wise and hardy. Then he chose men, so that the ship was well staffed, and said that he wanted to send a message to Ivar and the others to tell them of the fall of their father. But the journey seemed most hopeless, so that few wanted to go.

Then the king spoke: "Now you must attend closely to how each of the brothers reacts to these tidings. Then return home afterward, as soon as you are given fair winds." He had the ships prepared so that they needed nothing. Then they set forth, and they traveled well.

Meanwhile, the sons of Ragnar had been harrying in the Southern Kingdom. At last they turned their course to the Northernlands and planned to visit their kingdom, where Ragnar ruled. They did not yet know of his battle-journey or how it had had turned out, but they were very curious to know of the outcome. Then they journeyed across the south of the land, and everywhere, when men heard of the journey of the brothers, they deserted their towns and ferried their belongings off and fled away before them, so that the brothers could scarcely find food for their troops. One morning Bjorn Iron-Sides woke and spoke a verse:

> *The heath-falcon flies here*
> *each morning over these hearty towns;*
> *with lack of luck*
> *he might die of hunger.*
> *He should fare south o'er the sand*
> *where we let the dew from great blows*
> *flow from wounds,*
> *there where is the flowing of men's deaths.*

And he spoke another:

> *It was first that we journeyed*
> *to begin to hold Frey's play*
> *in Rome,*
> *where we had scant few troops.*
> *There I let my sword be drawn*
> *for the murder and manslaughter*
> *of those gray-beards;*
> *the eagle shrieks o'er the fallen slain.*

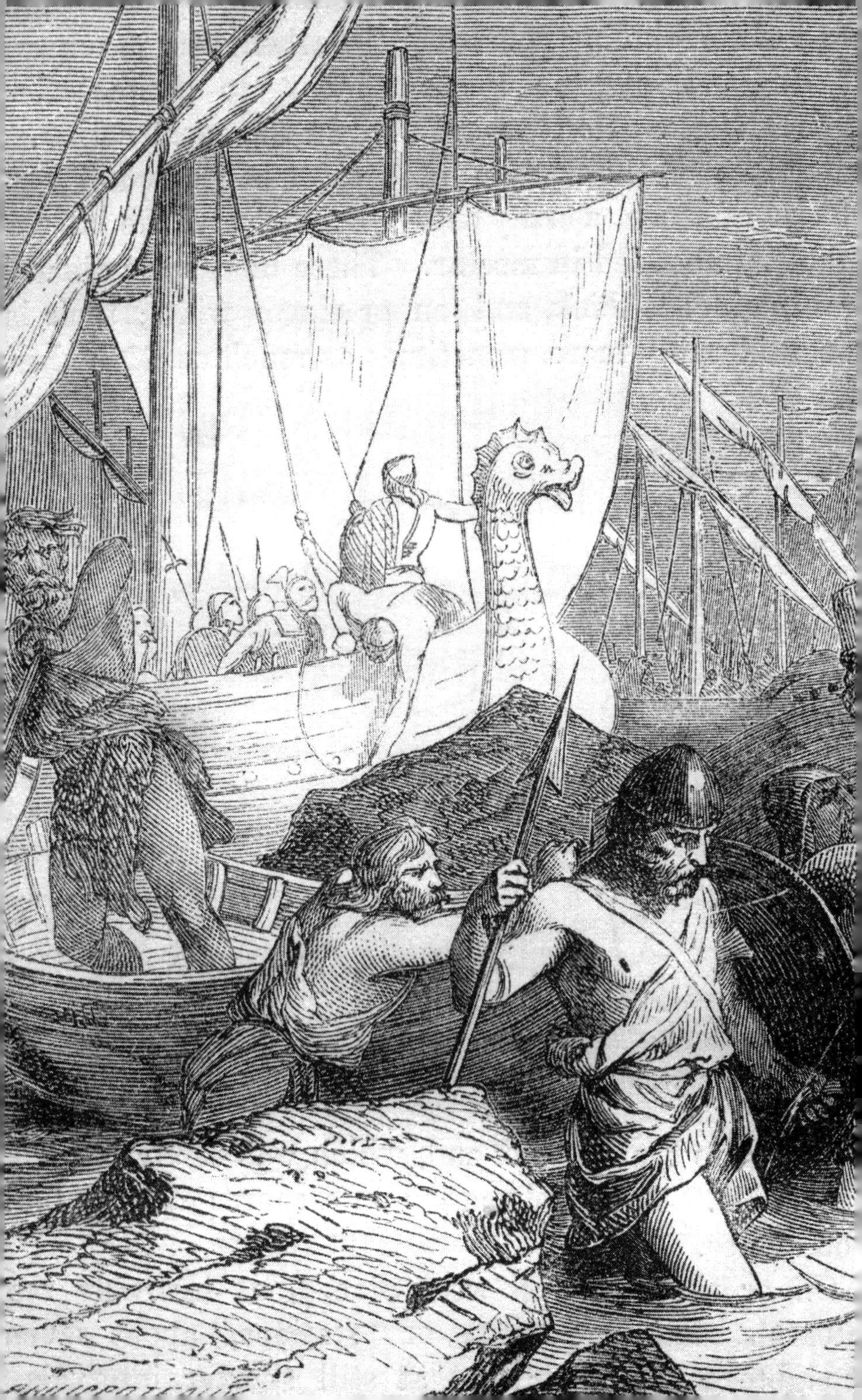

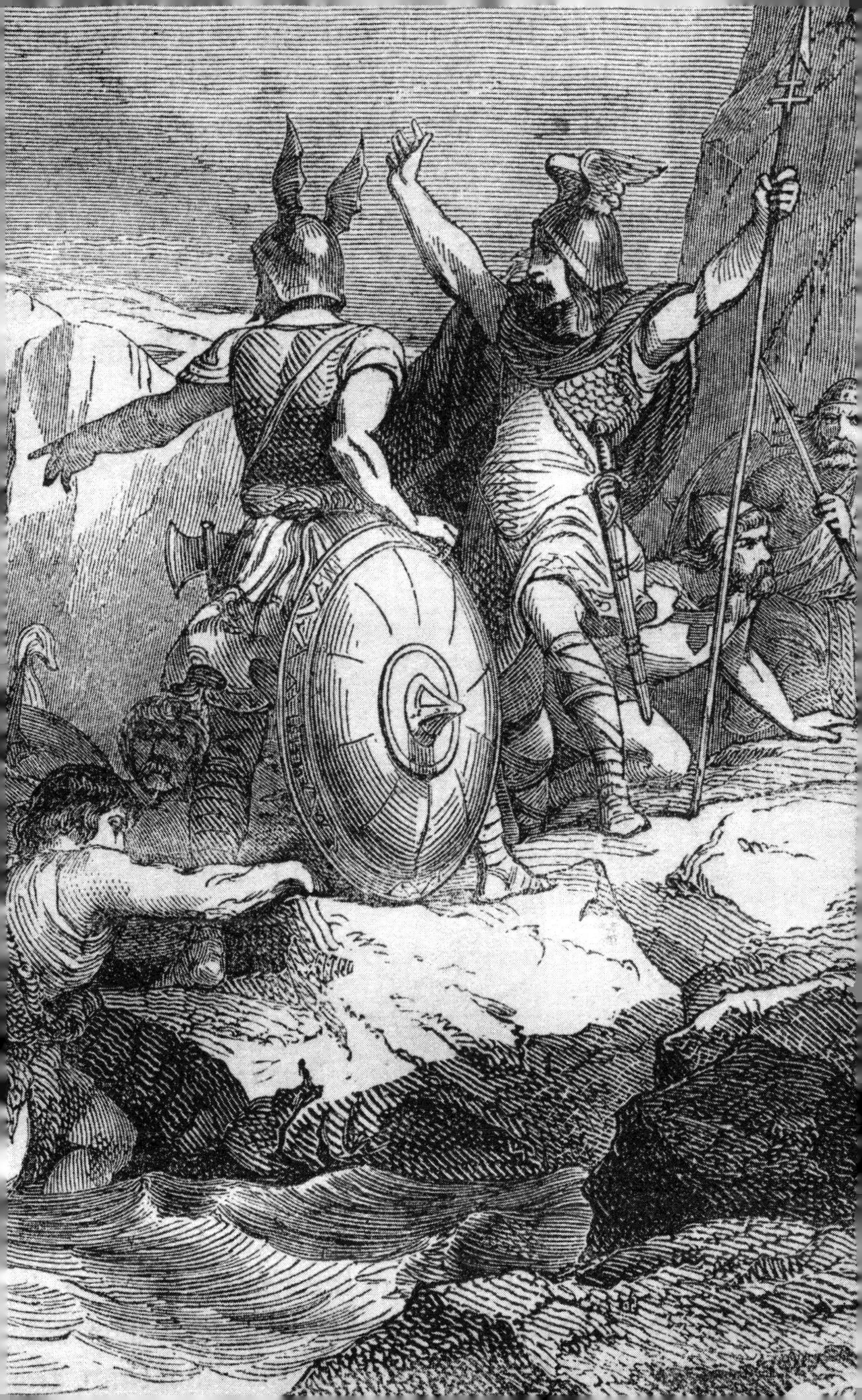

✣ XVI ✣

The brothers traveled on to Denmark, and arrived before the messengers of King Ella, and for a while they sat quietly with their troops. When the messengers came with their troops to the town where the sons of Ragnar were holding a feast, they entered the hall where they were drinking and stood before the high-seat where Ivar was lounging. Sigurd Worm-in-Eye and Hvitserk sat playing *hneftafl*, and Bjorn Iron-Sides was carving a spear-shaft on the floor of the hall. And when the messengers of King Ella came before Ivar, they spoke to him respectfully.

He received their greeting, and asked where they were from, and what tidings they bore. And the one, who was their leader, said that they were Englishmen, and that King Ella had sent them thither with tiding that spoke of the fall of Ragnar, their father. Hvitserk and Sigurd quickly let the *tafl*-pieces fall from their hands, and they attended closely to the tale. Bjorn stood on the floor of the hall and leaned on his spear-shaft. But Ivar asked them to relate exactly what the circumstances of Ragnar's life-leaving had been.

And so they told it all as it had happened, from the time he came to England until the time he gave up his life. Then, when the tale came to when Ragnar had said "the young boars might grumble," Bjorn squeezed the spear-shaft with his hand, and he squeezed so fiercely that the imprint of his hand was left on the haft afterward. When the messengers ended the recounting, Bjorn shook the spear asunder, so that it broke into two pieces. And Hvitserk held a *tafl*-piece that he had been moving, and he crushed it so strongly that blood spurted out from under each fingernail. And Sigurd Worm-in-Eye had been holding a knife and paring his nails when the tidings were being told, and he listened so closely to the tale that he did not notice that the knife slipped had cut clear to the bone, and he did not flinch. But Ivar asked again how it all had happened, and his color was now red, now livid, and he would suddenly become very pale, and he was so swollen that his flesh was all mortified from the anger that was in his breast. Then Hvitserk began to speak and said that vengeance could be most quickly achieved by killing the messengers sent from King Ella.

Ivar said: "That shall not be. They shall go in peace wherever they wish, and anything that they lack, they need only ask me for, and I shall secure it for them."

And when the messengers had ended their errand, they turned back out of the hall and returned to their ships. When the wind allowed, they put out to sea, and they traveled well until they returned to King Ella, and they told him how each of the brothers had reacted to the tidings. After King Ella heard from the messengers, he spoke: "It is certain that we will need fear either Ivar or else no one, because of what you say of him: thoughts of revenge do not run very deep in them, and we will manage to hold our kingdom against them." Then he had watchmen sent throughout all his kingdom, so that no army might come at him unknown.

When the messengers of King Ella had gone away, the brothers began to discuss how they should go about revenging Ragnar, their father. Then Ivar spoke: "I will have no part in this—I shall not muster troops, for it happened with Ragnar as I had thought it would. He prepared badly for his action from the beginning. He had no grievance with King Ella, and it often happens that if a man stubbornly decides to act unjustly, he is brought down in such a way. I, for one, will accept compensation from King Ella, if he will give it to me."

But when his brothers heard that, they became very angry and said that they would never act so cowardly, although he wished to.

"Many might say that we wrongly rest our hands upon our knees if we do not seek vengeance for our father, when before we have fared widely across the land with war-shields and killed many a guiltless man. But it shall not be so; rather every ship in Denmark that is seaworthy shall be readied. The most skilled troops shall be gathered, so that every man who may bear a shield against King Ella shall travel with us."

But Ivar said that he would leave behind all those ships that he commanded,—"except for that one, which I will be upon myself." And when the news spread that Ivar would not take any part in the action, they received many fewer troops, but the brothers went nonetheless. When they came to England, King Ella became aware of it and quickly had his trumpets sounded and called to him all the men who wished to assist him. Then he went with so many troops that no one could say how many had come, and he went to meet the brothers.

Then the armies met with each other, and Ivar was not there when they clashed in battle. And when the battle ended, it came about that the sons of Ragnar fled, and King Ella had the victory. And while the king was pursuing the fleeing host, Ivar told his brothers that he did not intend to turn back to his land—"for I desire to find out whether King Ella will do me any honor or not; it seems to me better to thus receive compensation from him than to be defeated again as we have now been."

Hvitserk said that he would not have dealings with King Ella, but Ivar could go about his affairs as he wished. "However, we shall never take payment for our father."

Ivar said that he would part with them, and told them to rule the kingdom that they had all held together, "and you should send me my things, when I ask for them." And when he had spoken, he bade them farewell. Then he turned away to meet with King Ella. And when Ivar came before him, he greeted the king worthily, and spoke to him thus: "I have come to meet with you, and I want to come to an agreement with you on such compensation as you will prepare for me. For now I see that I have nothing compared to you, and it seems to me better to accept such compensation from you as you will grant me, rather than to lose my men or myself to you."

Then King Ella answered: "Some men claim that it is not safe to trust you, and that you speak most fairly when you are thinking deceitfully. It would be difficult to defend against you and your brothers."

"I will ask little of you. If you will grant it, I will swear to you in this manner: that I shall never be against you." Then the king asked him to say what compensation he wanted. Ivar said, "I want you to give me as much of your land as an ox-hide covers, and outside of that shall be the outer boundary. I will not ask more from you, and I think that you would do me little honor if you will not grant me this."

"I do not know," said the king, "whether or not you can harm me if you have that much of my land, but I think I will give it to you nonetheless, if you will swear not to bear arms against me. If you are true to me, I shall not fear your brothers."

✠ XVII ✠

After they discussed the matter between the two of them, Ivar swore King Ella an oath that he would not strike against him and not conspire to cause him harm, and in return he should have as much of England as an oxhide could cover, the largest he might find.

Then Ivar took a hide from an old bull and he had it softened, and then he had it stretched three times. Then he cut it all asunder into strips, as narrowly as possible, and then he let them be split in half, between the hair and the flesh. And when this was done, the thong was so long that it was marveled at, as it had not been thought that it might become so large. And then he had it laid around a field, and there was as much space as was within a large town, and there he had the foundation marked for a large town-wall. Then he gathered to him many craftsmen and had many houses built upon on the field, and eventually he build an entire city, and it was called London. It is the largest and most famous of all towns in the Northern-Lands.

After he had this town built, he had his goods and valuables sent over. And he was so liberal that he gave gifts with both hands, and people thought so much of his wisdom that all sought his council and wanted him to settle the most difficult cases. He arranged all disputes in such a way that each party though he got the best of it, and he became popular, so that he had many friends about him. The king himself took advice from him, and he arranged the cases so that they did not come before the king at all. Ivar proceeded with his plan until it seemed that he was settled peacefully in England. Then he sent men to find his brothers and tell them that they should send him as much gold and silver as he asked for. When these messengers found the brothers, they told their message as well as what had come of Ivar's plan—namely, that they did not know what cunning he was preparing, but he was up to something.

As a result, the brothers thought that he was not as unmoved by their father's death as he had made it seem, so they sent such goods as he had asked for. And when the gold and silver came to Ivar, he gave gifts to all the strongest men in the land and so stole the troops out from under King Ella. They all promised Ivar that they would sit quiet, though he might later prepare for war. After Ivar had thus stolen the troops out from under the king, then he sent messengers to find his brothers and tell them that he wanted them to send a levy throughout all the lands under their rule, and they should demand however many men they could get. And when this message came to the brothers, they quickly figured out that he most likely thought it very promising that they might now gain victory in England. They summoned troops from all of Denmark and Gautland and all the kingdoms over which they held sway, and an innumerable host was gathered together when the assemblage was complete.

They then held course in their ships toward England both night and day, for they wanted to let as little forewarning of their coming to travel before them as possible. When rumours of war reached King Ella, he summoned his troops but few men came to him, because Ivar had stolen many troops out from under him. Then Ivar went and met King Ella and said that he would fulfill the oath that he had sworn not to bear arms against the king. "But I cannot influence my brothers' doings. However, I can try to find them and know if they might be willing stop their army and do no more ill than they have already done."

Then Ivar went to meet his brothers and encouraged them greatly to go forth as best they could and let a battle come about as soon as possible, "because the king has very few troops." And they answered that he did not need to encourage them, as their intent was the same as before. Then Ivar went and met King Ella and told him that they were too eager and enraged to listen to his words. "And when I wanted to bring peace between you, they shouted against it. Now I will carry through on my vow, that I would not war against you: I will be quiet along with my troops, and the battle with you may go as it will."

Then King Ella saw the troops of the brothers, and they came so fiercely that it was wondrous. Then Ivar spoke:

"Now is the time that you should prepare your troops, King Ella, and I think that they will press against you with a strong onslaught for a while." And as soon as the troops met each other there was a great battle, and the sons of Ragnar came hard upon the army of King Ella. Their vehemence was so great that their only thoughts were how they might work the most damage, and the war was both long and hard. And the battle ended thus—King Ella and his troops took to flight, but the king was seized.

Ivar was then nearby, and he said that they should now bring about his life-leaving. "Now is the time," he said, "to remember the manner of death that he inflicted on our father. Now a man who is most skilled in woodcarving shall mark an eagle on his back so precisely that the eagle shall run red with his blood."

And that man, when he was called to this task, did as Ivar commanded him, and King Ella was in great agony before the job was ended. Then he gave up his life, and it seemed to them that they then had vengeance for their father, Ragnar. Ivar said that he wanted to give them the kingdom that they all held together, as he wished to remain and rule over England.

✤ XVIII ✤

After that, Hvitserk and Bjorn journeyed home to their kingdom along with Sigurd, but Ivar stayed behind and ruled England. From then on they kept their troops together less, and harried separately in various lands. And Randalin, their mother, became an old woman. One time Hvitserk, her son, had gone raiding on his own in the Eastern Ways, but great forces came to meet him, so great that he could not raise his shield against them, and he was seized. And he then chose his manner of death: that a pyre should be made of the heads of his fallen troops, and there he would burn and thus give up his life. And when Randalin heard that, she spoke a verse:

One son which I had
endured death in Eastern Ways;
he was called Hvitserk,
who was never eager to flee.
He was heated on heads
hewed from those chosen at battle—
brave prince chose that
death before he fell.

Then she spoke another:

*The tree of the people
had himself destroyed
with countless heads under the king;
fingers of fire sang out his fate.
What better bed should
a battle-striker lay himself upon?
The high all-ruling chieftain
chose to fall with renown.*

A great family-line has come from Sigurd Worm-in-Eye. His daughter was called Ragnhild, the mother of Harald Fairhair, the first to conquer all of of Norway and rule it as one kingdom.

Ivar ruled over England until his dying day, when he became deathly sick. And when he lay with that killing-illness, he said that he should be laid to rest by the shore where the land was most exposed to raiders, and he said if that was done then any who would land there would not gain victory. And when he breathed his last, it was done as he had said, and he was then laid in a cairn overlooking the sea. And many men say that when King Harold Sigurdarson arrived in England, he arrived where Ivar was, and that is why he fell on that expedition. And when William the Conqueror came to England, he went and broke open Ivar's cairn and saw Ivar's corpse unrotten. Then he had a great fire made and had Ivar's body burned in the fire, and after that he battled across the land and had victory.

And from Bjorn Iron-Sides have come many men. From him has come a great family: Thorth who farmed at Hoftha in Hofthastrond, was a great leader at the *moots*.

And then when the sons of Ragnar had all given up their lives, their troops who had assisted them were dispersed far and wide, and all of them who had been with the sons of Ragnar thought that there was no worth in other princes. There were two men who traveled widely across the land to discover if they could find any prince whom they thought it would not be disgraceful for them to serve, but they did not travel together.

☩ XIX ☩

It came to pass that a certain king had two sons. He took sick and breathed his last, and his sons wished to drink a funeral feast for him. They decreed that all men could come there to the feast that had heard of it, and they would hold the feast after three winters had passed. Now this news was heard widely throughout the land. For three winters they prepared the feast, and when the summer came when they would drink the funeral feast and the time that had been appointed arrived, the feast turned out to be so very filled with men that none knew of its precedent it was so large, and many great halls were prepared and many tents set up outside.

And when they were well into the first evening, a man came into the hall. This man was so large that none were as large as he, and from his attire it could be seen that he had been with noble men. And when he came into the hall, he went before the brothers and spoke to them and asked where they would have him to sit. They were pleased by his appearance, and so they told him to sit on the upper bench. He needed the space of two men. And as soon as he had sat down, drink was brought to him as to other men, but there was not a horn so large that he might not drink it off in one drink, and all thought they could tell that they were all as nothing compared to him.

Then it happened that another man came to the feast. He was considerably larger than the one who came before. Both men wore low-hanging hoods. And when this man came before the high-seat of the young kings, he spoke handsomely and asked them to direct him to a seat. They said that this man should sit on the upper bench as well, but even farther in than the other. Now he took his seat, and together they took up so much room that five men had to rise up for them. And he who came first was the smaller drinker, as the second one drank so quickly that he poured nearly every horn into himself, and men did not find that he became drunk. It seemed he held his seat-mate in contempt, as he turned his back to the other large man. Then he who came first said that they should have a game together—"and I will go first." He shoved the other with his hand and spoke a verse:

Speak of your great achievements,
educate us, I ask you—
have you seen the ravens shudder
on the branch, bloated with blood?
You have more often been otherwise:
found in the high-seat
rather than gathering bloody carrion
for birds of war in the dale!

Now it seemed to the other that he was challenged by such a direct verse, and he spoke a verse in reply:

Be silent at once, you called a stay-at-home;
you are content with very little,
you have never done
what I may boast of!
You have not fattened

*the sun-seeking-bitch with the drink
of sword's play, but gave up the harbor horses;
what is troubling you?*

Now he who came first answered:

*We let the strong cheek
of the horses of the sea
run to the waves, the sides of
our bright mail splattered with blood.
The she-wolf feasted, the hunger
of the eagles was sated on the
blood from men's reddened necks,
while we seized the hard meal of the fish's land.*

Now he who came second spoke:

*Very little I saw of you
when the swift
wading horses found the
brewing white plain before them;
and with weak courage
you hid from the ravens, near the mast,
when we turned our red-prows
again to the land.*

And then the one who came first spoke:

It does us no honor
to quarrel about what we have done
greater than the other,
over ale in the high-seat.
You stood upon the sword-stag
as waves bore it through the sound,
and I sat in the birth as the
red prow rode into harbor.

Now he who came second answered:

We were both companions
of Bjorn at the sword-din,
we were proven warriors
when we strove for Ragnar;
I bear the wound in my side
from the heroes' beaks
in the land of the Bolgars—
neighbor, sit further in beside me!

In the end they knew each other and were together there at the feast.

✠ XX ✠

There was a man named Ogmund, who was called Ogmund The Dane. He journeyed one day along with five ships, and lay anchor at Samsey in Munarvag. Then it is said that the cooks went to land to prepare the meat, and other men went into the woods to entertain themselves. There they found an ancient wooden statue carved in the shape of man. It was forty feet in height and covered with moss, but they could still make out all of him, and they discussed among themselves who might have sacrificed to this great god. And then the tree-man spoke:

> *It was long ago*
> *when the offspring*
> *of the sea-king journeyed*
> *on the way here*
> *in the tongues of landings*
> *across the bright salty trail;*
> *since then, I have been responsible*
> *for guarding this place.*
> *And so the warriors,*
> *sons of Lothbrok,*
> *set me thus*
> *near the southern salt-sea;*
> *in the southern parts*

*of Samsey they sacrificed
to me, prayed for
the deaths of men.
They bade me
stand near the thorn-bush,
covered in moss,
as long as the strand endured.
Clouds weep upon
each of my cheeks,
for now neither flesh
nor clothing shelters me.*

And that seemed wondrous to them, and afterward they told the tale far and wide.

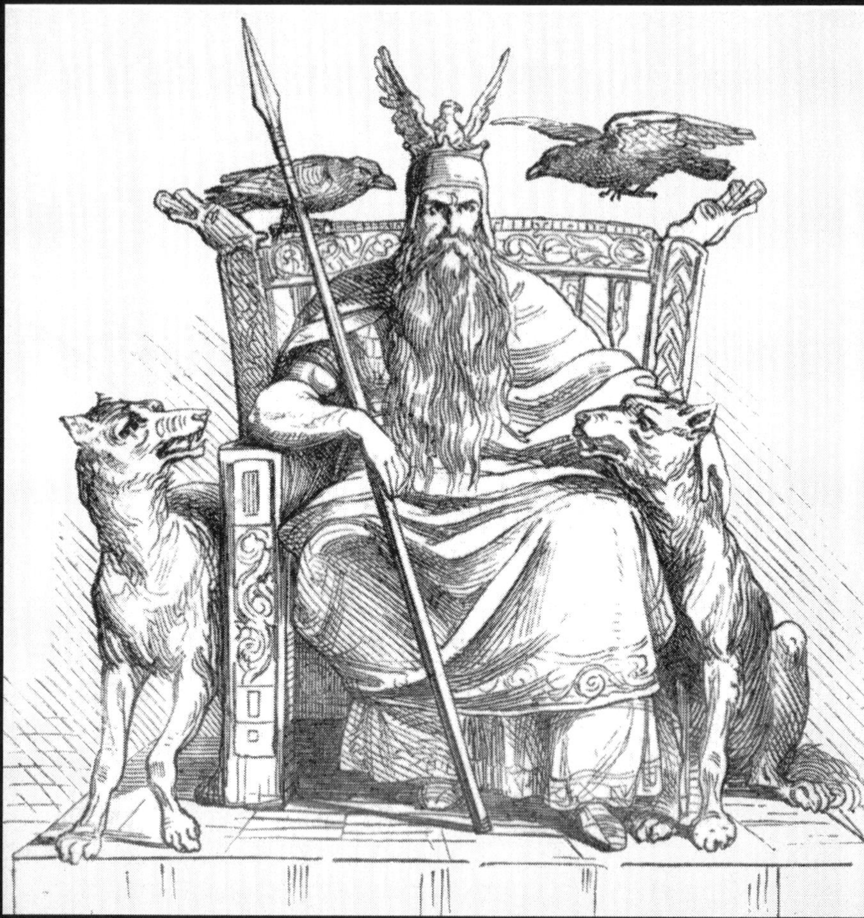

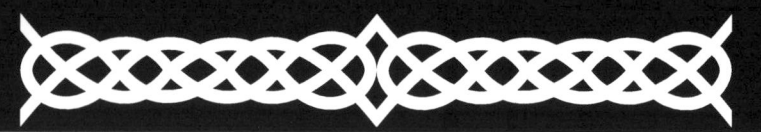

THE ANGLO-SAXON CHRONICLE
PART 2: A.D. 750–919

(Notes added in italic.)

A.D. 845. This year Alderman Eanwulf, with the men of Somersetshire, and Bishop Ealstan, and Alderman Osric, with the men of Dorsetshire, fought at the mouth of the Parret with the Danish army; and there, after making a great slaughter, obtained the victory.

Note: The Danish army mentioned here is said to be led by Ragnar.

A.D. 851. This year Alderman Ceorl, with the men of Devonshire, fought the heathen army at Wemburg, and after making great slaughter obtained the victory. The same year King Athelstan and Alderman Elchere fought in their ships, and slew a large army at Sandwich in Kent, taking nine ships and dispersing the rest. The heathens now for the first time remained over winter in the Isle of Thanet. The same year came three hundred and fifty ships into the mouth of the Thames; the crew of which went upon land, and stormed Canterbury and London; putting to flight Bertulf, king of the Mercians, with his army; and then marched southward over the Thames into Surrey. Here Ethelwulf and his son Ethelbald, at the head of the West-Saxon army, fought with them at Ockley, and made the greatest slaughter of the heathen army that we have ever heard reported to this present day. There also they obtained the victory.

Note: While Ragnar is not credited with this raid, it fits into the timeline used by Vikings *seasons 1 and 2.*

A.D. 854. This year the heathen men for the first time remained over winter in the Isle of Shepey. The same year King Ethelwulf registered a TENTH of his land over all his kingdom for the honor of God and for his own everlasting salvation. The same year also he went to Rome with great pomp, and was resident there a twelvemonth. Then he returned homeward; and Charles, king of the Franks, gave him his daughter, whose name was Judith, to be his queen. After this he came to his people, and they were fain to receive him; but about two years after his residence among the Franks he died; and his body lies at Winchester. He reigned eighteen years and a half. [...] Then two sons of Ethelwulf succeeded to the kingdom; Ethelbald to Wessex, and Ethelbert to Kent, Essex, Surrey, and Sussex. Ethelbald reigned five years. Alfred, his third son, Ethelwulf had sent to Rome; and when the pope heard say that he was dead, he consecrated Alfred king, and held him under spiritual hands, as his father Ethelwulf had desired, and for which purpose he had sent him thither.

Note: This entry tells of King Alfred's father, Æthelwulf, who is featured in season 3 of Vikings. *Here he is married to King Charles of France's daughter, Judith. She is also featured in season 3 of* Vikings. *It also relates the consecration of a young Alfred in Rome by the pope.*

A.D. 865. This year sat the heathen army in the isle of Thanet, and made peace with the men of Kent, who promised money therewith; but under the security of peace, and the promise of money, the army in the night stole up the country, and overran all Kent eastward.

Note: This entry marks the arrival of the Ragnarssons in England. By this time, Ragnar has been killed. Ragnar's sons have come to England, according to legend, on a mission to avenge the death of their father.

Note: Everything that follows tells of the Viking invasion, Alfred's rise to the throne, and the ensuing battles with the Vikings.

A.D. 866. This year Ethelred, brother of Ethelbert, took to the West-Saxon government; and the same year came a large heathen army into England, and fixed their winter-quarters in East-Anglia, where they were soon horsed; and the inhabitants made peace with them.

A.D. 867. This year the army went from the East-Angles over the mouth of the Humber to the Northumbrians, as far as York. And there was much dissension in that nation among themselves; they had deposed their king Osbert, and had admitted Aella, who had no natural claim. Late in the year, however, they returned to their allegiance, and they were now fighting against the common enemy; having collected a vast force, with which they fought the army at York; and breaking open the town, some of them entered in. Then was there an immense slaughter of the Northumbrians, some within and some without; and both the kings were slain on the spot. The survivors made peace with the army. The same year Bishop Ealstan died, who had the bishopric of Sherborn fifty winters, and his body lies in the town.

A.D. 868. This year the same army went into Mercia to Nottingham, and there fixed their winter-quarters; and Burhred, king of the Mercians, with his council, besought Ethelred, king of the West-Saxons, and Alfred, his brother; that they would assist them in fighting against the army. And they went with the West-Saxon army into Mercia as far as Nottingham, and there meeting the army on the works, they beset them within. But there was no heavy fight; for the Mercians made peace with the army.

A.D. 869. This year the army went back to York, and sat there a year.

A.D. 870. This year the army rode over Mercia into East-Anglia, and there fixed their winter-quarters at Thetford. And in the winter King Edmund fought with them; but the Danes gained the victory, and slew the king; whereupon they overran all that land, and destroyed all the monasteries to which they came. The names of the leaders who slew the king were Hingwar and Hubba. At the same time came they to Medhamsted, burning and breaking, and slaying abbot and monks, and all that they there found. They made such havoc there, that a monastery, which was before full rich, was now reduced to nothing. The same year died Archbishop Ceolnoth; and Ethelred, Bishop of Witshire, was chosen Archbishop of Canterbury.

Note: This entry references Ubbe and Ivar the Boneless specifically. They are responsible for slaying King Edmund, who becomes a martyred saint in England.

A.D. 871. This year came the army to Reading in Wessex; and in the course of three nights after rode two earls up, who were met by Alderman Ethelwulf at Englefield; where he fought with them, and obtained the victory. There one of them was slain, whose name was Sidrac. About four nights after this, King Ethelred and Alfred his brother led their main army to Reading, where they fought with the enemy; and there was much slaughter on either hand, Alderman

Ethelwulf being among the slain; but the Danes kept possession of the field. And about four nights after this, King Ethelred and Alfred his brother fought with all the army on Ashdown, and the Danes were overcome. They had two heathen kings, Bagsac and Healfden, and many earls; and they were in two divisions; in one of which were Bagsac and Healfden, the heathen kings, and in the other were the earls. King Ethelred therefore fought with the troops of the kings, and there was King Bagsac slain; and Alfred his brother fought with the troops of the earls, and there were slain Earl Sidrac the elder, Earl Sidrac the younger, Earl Osbern, Earl Frene, and Earl Harold. They put both the troops to flight; there were many thousands of the slain, and they continued fighting till night. Within a fortnight of this, King Ethelred and Alfred his brother fought with the army at Basing; and there the Danes had the victory. About two months after this, King Ethelred and Alfred his brother fought with the army at Marden. They were in two divisions; and they put them both to flight, enjoying the victory for some time during the day; and there was much slaughter on either hand; but the Danes became masters of the field; and there was slain Bishop Heahmund, with many other good men. After this fight came a vast army in the summer to Reading. And after the Easter of this year died King Ethelred. He reigned five years, and his body lies at Winburnminster. Then Alfred, his brother, the son of Ethelwulf, took to the kingdom of Wessex. And within a month of this, King Alfred fought against all the Army with a small force at Wilton, and long pursued them during the day; but the Danes got possession of the field. This year were nine general battles fought with the army in the kingdom south of the Thames; besides those skirmishes, in which Alfred the king's brother, and every single alderman, and the thanes of the king, oft rode against them; which were accounted nothing. This year also were slain nine earls, and one king; and the same year the West-Saxons made peace with the army.

Note: In this entry, Alfred takes the throne of Wessex. He continues the battle against the Vikings.

A.D. 872. This year went the army to London from Reading, and there chose their winter-quarters. Then the Mercians made peace with the army.

A.D. 873. This year went the army against the Northumbrians, and fixed their winter-quarters at Torksey in Lindsey. And the Mercians again made peace with the army.

A.D. 874. This year went the army from Lindsey to Repton, and there took up their winter-quarters, drove the king, Burhred, over sea, when he had reigned about two and twenty winters, and subdued all that land. He then went to Rome, and there remained to the end of his life.

And his body lies in the church of Sancta Maria, in the school of the English nation. And the same year they gave Ceolwulf, an unwise king's thane, the Mercian kingdom to hold; and he swore oaths to them, and gave hostages, that it should be ready for them on whatever day they would have it; and he would be ready with himself, and with all those that would remain with him, at the service of the army.

A.D. 875. This year went the army from Repton; and Healfden advanced with some of the army against the Northumbrians, and fixed his winter-quarters by the river Tine. The army then subdued that land, and oft invaded the Picts and the Strathclydwallians. Meanwhile the three kings, Guthrum, Oskytel, and Anwind, went from Repton to Cambridge with a vast army, and sat there one year. This summer King Alfred went out to sea with an armed fleet, and fought with seven ship-rovers, one of whom he took, and dispersed the others.

Note: This entry tells how Halfdan Ragnarsson raided and conquered in the north. Halfdan has not yet appeared in Vikings.

A.D. 876. This year Rollo penetrated Normandy with his army; and he reigned fifty winters. And this year the army stole into Wareham, a fort of the West-Saxons. The king afterward made peace with them; and they gave him as hostages those who were worthiest in the army; and swore with oaths on the holy bracelet, which they would not before to any nation, that they would readily go out of his kingdom. Then, under color of this, their cavalry stole by night into Exeter. The same year Healfden divided the land of the Northumbrians; so that they became afterwards their harrowers and plowers.

Note: This entry references Rollo's invasion of Normandy. Note that Ragnar is long dead when the historical Rollo, who is no relation of Ragnar's, establishes himself in France. Halfdan's campaigns are also described.

A.D. 876. And in this same year the army of the Danes in England swore oaths to King Alfred upon the holy ring, which before they would not do to any nation; and they delivered to the king hostages from among the most distinguished men of the army, that they would speedily depart from his kingdom; and that by night they broke.

A.D. 877. This year came the Danish army into Exeter from Wareham; while the navy sailed west about, until they met with a great mist at sea, and there perished one hundred and twenty ships at Swanwich. Meanwhile King Alfred with his army rode after the cavalry as far as Exeter; but he could not overtake them before their arrival in the fortress, where they could not be come at. There they gave him as many hostages as he required, swearing with solemn oaths to observe the strictest amity. In the harvest the army entered Mercia; some of which they divided among them, and some they gave to Ceolwulf.

A.D. 878. This year about mid-winter, after twelfth-night, the Danish army stole out to Chippenham, and rode over the land of the West-Saxons; where they settled, and drove many of the people over sea; and of the rest the greatest part they rode down, and subdued to their will; —ALL BUT ALFRED THE KING. He, with a little band, uneasily sought the woods and fastnesses of the moors. And in the winter of this same year the brother of Ingwar and Healfden landed in Wessex, in Devonshire, with three and twenty ships, and there was he slain, and eight hundred men with him, and forty of his army. There also was taken the war-flag, which they called the RAVEN. In the Easter of this year King Alfred with his little force raised a work at Athelney; from that he assailed the army, assisted by that part of Somersetshire that was nighest to it. Then, in the seventh week after Easter, he rode to Brixton by the eastern side of Selwood; and there came out to meet him all the people of Somersersetshire, and Wiltshire, and that part of Hampshire that is on this side of the sea; and they rejoiced to see him. Then within one night he went from this retreat to Hey; and within one night after he proceeded to Heddington; and there fought with all the army, and put them to flight, riding after them as far as the fortress, where he remained a fortnight. Then the army gave him hostages with many oaths, that they would go out of his kingdom. They told him also, that their king would receive baptism. And they acted accordingly; for in the course of three weeks after, King Guthrum, attended by some thirty of the worthiest men that were in the army, came to him at Aller, which is near Athelney, and there the king became his sponsor in baptism; and his crisom-leasing was at Wedmor. He was there twelve nights with the king, who honored him and his attendants with many presents.

Note: This entry describes the Treaty of Alfred and Guthrum, an agreement that established the division of England into Danish and Anglo-Saxon territories.

A.D. 901. This year died ALFRED, the son of Ethelwulf, six nights before the mass of All Saints. He was king over all the English nation, except that part that was under the power of the Danes. He held the government one year and a half less than thirty winters; and then Edward, his son, took to the government. Then Prince Ethelwald, the son of his paternal uncle, rode against the towns of Winburn and of Twineham, without leave of the king and his council. Then rode the king with his army; so that he encamped the same night at Badbury near Winburn; and Ethelwald remained within the town with the men that were under him, and had all the gates shut upon him, saying, that he would either there live or there die. But in the meantime he stole away in the night, and sought the army in Northumberland. The king gave orders to ride after him; but they were not able to overtake him. The Danes, however, received him as their king. They then rode after the wife that Ethelwald had taken without the king's leave, and against the command of the bishops; for she was formerly consecrated a nun. In this year also died Ethelred, who was alderman of Devonshire, four weeks before King Alfred.

Note: This entry reports the death of King Alfred.

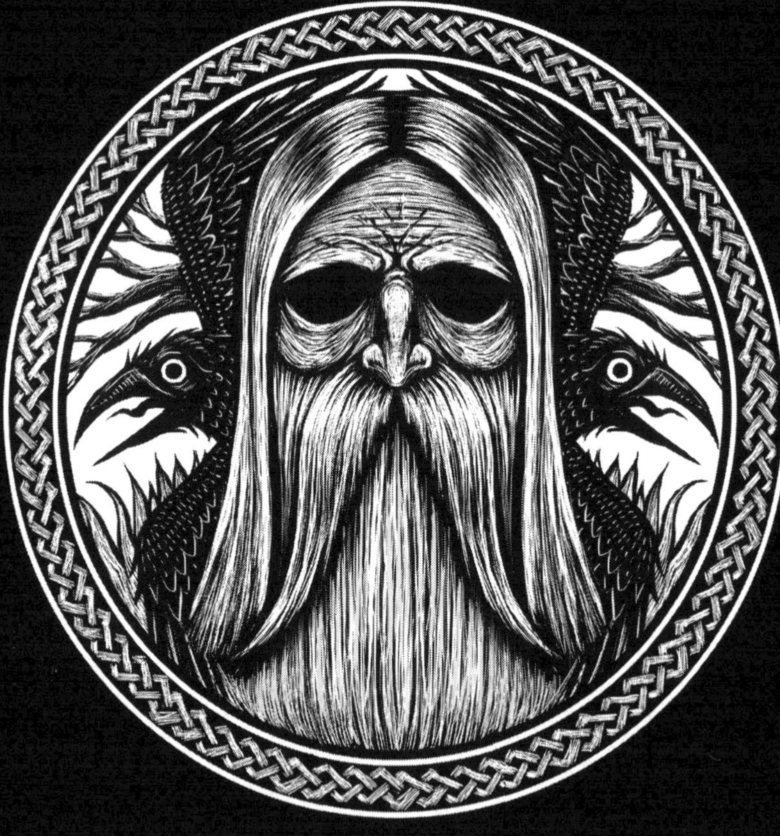

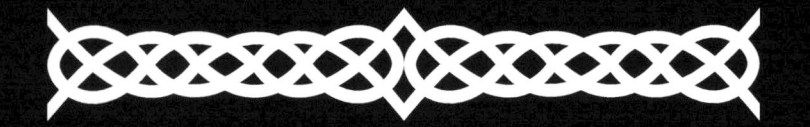

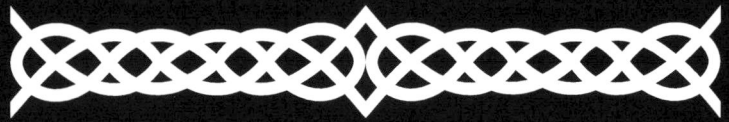

KRÁKUMÁL
THE DYING ODE OF RAGNAR LOTHBROK
12TH CENTURY A.D.

INTRODUCTION

King Ragnar Lothbrok was a celebrated Poet, Warrior, and (what was the same thing in those ages) Pirate; who reigned in Denmark, about the beginning of the ninth century. After many warlike expeditions by sea and land, he at length met with bad fortune. He was taken in battle by his adversary Ella king of Northumberland. War in those rude ages was carried on with the fame inhumanity, as it is now among the savages of North America: their prisoners were only reserved to be put to death with torture. Ragnar was accordingly thrown into a dungeon to be stung to death by serpents. While he was dying he composed this song, wherein he records all the valiant achievements of his life, and threatens Ella with vengeance; which history informs us was afterwards executed by the sons of Ragnar. [3]

It is, after all, conjectured that Ragnar himself only composed a few stanzas of this poem, and that the rest were added by his *Scald* or poet-laureat, whose business it was to add to the solemnities of his funeral by singing some poem in his praise. *L'Edda par Chev. Mallet, p.* 150

This piece is translated from the Islandic original published by Olaus Wormius in his *Literatura Runica Hafniæ* *4to.*1631.—*Ibidem,* 2. *Edit. Fol.* 1651.

N. B. Thora, mentioned in the first stanza, was daughter of some little Gothic prince, whose palace was infested by a large serpent; he offered his daughter in marriage to any one that would kill the monster and set her free. Ragnar accomplished the atchievement and acquired the name of *Lod-brog,* which signifies ROUGH or HAIRY-BREECHES, because he cloathed himself all over in rough or hairy skins before he made the attack. [*Vide Saxon Gram. pages* 152, 153.]—This is the poetical account of this adventure: but history informs us that Thora was kept prisoner by one of her father's vassals, whose name was *Orme* or SERPENT, and that it was from this man that Ragnar delivered her, clad in the aforesaid shaggy armour. But he himself chuses to commemorate it in the most poetical manner.

Vide Chev. Mallet Introd. a L'Hist. de Dannemarc. page 201.

✢ I ✢

We fought with swords: when in Gothland I slew an enormous serpent: my reward was the beauteous Thora. Thence I was deemed a man: they called me Lothbrok from that slaughter. I thrust the monster through with my spear, with the steel productive of splendid rewards. [4]

✢ II ✢

We fought with swords: I was very young, when toward the East, in the straights of Eirar, we gained rivers of blood* for the ravenous wolf: ample food for the yellow-footed fowl.** There the hard iron sung upon the lofty helmets. The whole ocean was one wound. The raven waded in the blood of the slain.

✢ III ✢

We fought with swords: we lifted high our lances; when I had numbered twenty years, and everywhere acquired

---

* Literally "Rivers of wounds."—By the yellow-footed fowl is meant the eagle.

** The eagle.

great renown. We conquered eight barons at the mouth of the Danube. We procured ample entertainment for the eagle in that slaughter. Bloody sweat fell in the ocean of wounds. A host of men there lost their lives.

✠ IV ✠

We fought with swords: we enjoyed the fight, when we sent the inhabitants of Helsing to the habitation of the gods.[*] We sailed up the Vistula. Then the sword acquired spoils: the whole ocean was one wound: the earth grew red with reeking gore: the sword grinned at the coats of mail: the sword cleft the shields asunder.

✠ V ✠

We fought with swords: I well remember that no one fled that day in the battle before in the ships Herauder [5] fell. There does not a fairer warrior divide the ocean with his vessels. This prince ever brought to the battle a gallant heart.

✠ VI ✠

We fought with swords: the army cast away their shields. Then flew the spear to the breasts of the warriors. The sword in the fight cut the very rocks: the shield was all besmeared with blood, before king Rafno fell, our foe.

---

[*] Literally, "to the hall of Odin."

The warm sweat run down from the heads on the coats of mail.

✣ VII ✣

We fought with swords, before the isles of Indir. We gave ample prey for the ravens to rend in pieces: a banquet for the wild beasts that feed on flesh. At that time all were valiant: it were difficult to single out any one. At the rising of the sun, I saw the lances pierce: the bows darted the arrows from them.

✣ VIII ✣

We fought with swords: loud was the din* of arms; before king Eistin fell in the field.

Thence, enriched with golden spoils, we marched to fight in the land of Vals. There the sword cut the painted shields.** In the meeting of helmets, the blood ran from the wounds: it ran down from the cloven sculls of men.

✣ IX ✣

We fought with swords, before Boring-holmi. We held bloody shields: we stained our spears. Showers of arrows brake the shield in pieces. The bow sent forth the glittering

---

* DIN is the word in the Islandic original. *Dinn greniudu brottan*. [6]

** Literally, "the paintings of the shields."

steel. Volnir fell in the conflict, than whom there was not a greater king. Wide on the shores lay the scattered dead: the wolves rejoiced over their prey.

✣ X ✣

We fought with swords, in the Flemings land: the battle widely raged before king Freyr fell therein. The blue steel all reeking with blood fell at length upon the golden mail. Many a virgin bewailed the laughter of that morning. The beasts of prey had ample spoil.

✣ XI ✣

We fought with swords, before Ainglanes. There saw I thousands lie dead in the ships: we sailed to the battle for six days before the army fell. There we celebrated a *mass of weapons*.* At rising of the sun Valdiofur fell before our swords.

✣ XII ✣

We fought with swords, at Bardafyrda. A mower of blood rained from our weapons. Headlong fell the palid corpse a

---

* This is intended for a sneer on the Christian religion, which tho' it had not gained any footing in the northern nations, when this Ode was written, was not wholly unknown to them. Their piratical expeditions into the southern countries had given them some notion of it, but by no means a favorable one: they considered it as the religion of cowards, because it would have corrected their savage manners.

prey for the hawks. The bow gave a twanging sound. The blade sharply bit the coats of mail: it bit the helmet in the fight. The arrow sharp with poison and all besprinkled with bloody sweat ran to the wound.

✠ XIII ✠

We fought with swords, before the bay of Hiadning. We held aloft magic shields in the play of battle. Then might you see men, who rent shields with their swords. The helmets were mattered in the murmur of the warriors. The pleasure of that day was like having a fair virgin placed beside one in the bed. [7]

✠ XIV ✠

We fought with swords, in the Northumbrian land. A furious storm descended on the shields: many a lifeless body fell to the earth. It was about the time of the morning, when the foe was compelled to fly in the battle. There the sword sharply bit the polished helmet. The pleasure of that day was like killing a young widow at the highest feat of the table.

✠ XV ✠

We fought with swords, in the isles of the south. There Herthiose proved victorious: there died many of our valiant warriors. In the mower of arms Rogvaldur fell: I lost my son. In the play of arms came the deadly spear: his lofty crest was dyed with gore. The birds of prey bewailed his fall: they loft him that prepared them banquets.

✣ XVI ✣

We fought with swords, in the Irish plains. The bodies of the warriors lay intermingled. The hawk rejoiced at the play of swords. The Irish king did not act the part of the eagle. Great was the conflict of sword and shield. King Marstan was killed in the bay: he was given a prey to the hungry ravens.

✣ XVII ✣

We fought with swords: the spear resounded: the banners shone* upon the coats of mail. I saw many a warrior fall in the morning: many a hero in the contention of arms. Here the sword reached betimes the heart of my son: it was Egill deprived Agnar of life. He was a youth, who never knew what it was to fear.

✣ XVIII ✣

We fought with swords, at Skioldunga. We kept our words: we carved out with our weapons a plenteous banquet for the wolves of the sea.** The ships were all besmeared with crim-

---

* Or more properly "reflected the sunshine up on the coat of mail."

** A poetical name for the fishes of prey.

son, as if for many days the maidens had brought and poured forth wine. All rent was the mail in the clash of arms.

✠ XIX ✠

We fought with swords, when Harold fell. I saw him struggling in the twilight of death; that young chief so proud of his flowing locks*: he who spent his mornings among the young maidens: he who loved to converse with the handsome widows.

✠ XX ✠

We fought with swords: we fought three kings in the isle of Lindis. Few had reason to rejoice that day. Many fell into the jaws of the wild-beasts. The hawk and the wolf tore the flesh of the dead: they departed glutted with their prey. The blood of the Irish fell plentifully into the ocean, during the time of that slaughter.

✠ XXI ✠

We fought with swords, at the isle of Onlug. The uplifted weapon bit the shields. The gilded lance grated on the mail. The traces of that fight will be seen for ages. There kings marched up to the play of arms. The mores of the sea were stained with blood. The lances appeared like flying dragons.

---

* He means Harold Harfax King of Norway. —*Harfax* (synonymous to our English *Fairfax*) signifies *Fair-locks*. [8]

✤ XXII ✤

We fought with swords. Death is the happy portion of the brave[*], for he stands the foremost against the storm of weapons. He, who flies from danger, often bewails his miserable life. Yet how difficult is it to rouse up a coward to the play of arms? The dastard feels no heart in his bosom.

✤ XXIII ✤

We fought with swords. Young men should march up to the conflict of arms: man should meet man and never give way. In this hath always consisted the nobility of the warrior. He, who aspires to the love of his mistress, ought to be dauntless in the clash of arms.

✤ XXIV ✤

We fought with swords. Now I find for certain that we are drawn along by fate. Who can evade the decrees of destiny? Could I have thought the conclusion of my life reserved for Ella; when almost expiring I shed torrents of blood? When I launched forth my ships into the deep? When in the Scottish gulphs I gained large spoils for the wolves?

---

[*] The northern warriors thought none were intitled to Elizium, but such as died in battle, or underwent a violent death.

✢ XXV ✢

We fought with swords: this fills me still with joy, because I know a banquet is preparing by the father of the gods. Soon, in the splendid hall of Odin, we shall drink beer* out of the sculls of our enemies. [9] A brave man shrinks not at death. I shall utter no repining words as I approach the palace of the gods. [10]

✢ XXVI ✢

We fought with swords. O that the sons of Aslauga** knew; O that my children knew the sufferings of their father! That numerous serpents filled with poison tear me to pieces! Soon would they be here: soon would they wage bitter war with their swords. I gave a mother to my children from whom they inherit a valiant heart.

✢ XXVII ✢

We fought with swords. Now I touch on my last moments. I receive a deadly hurt from the viper. A serpent inhabits the hall of my heart. Soon all my sons black their swords in the blood of Ella. They wax red with fury: they burn with rage. Those gallant youths will not rest till they have avenged their father.

---

* Beer and mead were the only nectar of the northern nations. Odin alone of all the gods was supposed to drink WINE. *Vid. Bartholin.*

** Aslauga was his second wife, whom he married after the death of Thora.

✠ XVIII ✠

We fought with swords. Battles fifty and one have been fought under my banners. From my early youth I learned to dye my sword in crimson: I never yet could find a king more valiant than myself. The gods now invite me to them. Death is not to be lamented.

✠ XXIX ✠

'Tis with joy I cease. The goddesses of destiny are come to fetch me. Odin hath sent them from the habitation of the gods. I mail be joyfully received into the highest seat; I mall quaff full goblets among the gods. The hours of my life are past away. I die laughing. [11]

NOTES

[1] For a general overview, see Kathryn Sutherland, "The Native Poet: The Influence of Percy's Minstrel from Beattie to Wordsworth", *Review of English Studies* 33 (1982): 414–33.

[2] Source: *Lodbrokar-Quida; or the Death Song of Lodbrok, Now First Correctly Printed from Various Manuscripts*, ed. James Johnstone (Copenhagen, 1782), 95–111.

[3] This revenge, Anglo-Saxon and Scandinavian histories tell us, took place when warriors, who are said to be Ragnar's sons, invaded northeast England in 867.

[4] The first stanza, about the victory over a supernatural creature, is strangely out of sync with the descriptions of ordinary, human battles enumerated in the rest of the poem. It was likely introduced as part of a different tradition associated with Ragnar. In Percy's essay "On Ancient Metrical Romances &c", prefixed to the third volume of *Reliques of Ancient English Poetry*, Percy used Ragnar's one-off knightly achievement in this stanza as evidence of English metrical romances being founded on Norse tradition. He says this despite the fact that the poem does not otherwise refer to Ragnar in connection with any romantic endeavors.

[5] Ragnar's father-in-law.

[6] This editorial note on the similarity between the Norse *dinn* and the English *din* appears to give no essential information to the reader apart from highlighting the closeness of Percy's translation to the original. It may also serve to back up his claim in the preface to *Five Pieces*, in which he speaks of the near affinity between Norse and Anglo-Saxon tradition, referring to Icelandic as a "sister dialect" of English. However, the annotation is based on a misreading. Percy's source, Worm's *Literatura runica*, had *Hett greniudu hrottar*. This is also how the line is rendered in the transcript of the Icelandic original which Percy included in the appendix to his anthology.

[7] The apparent continuity between Ragnar's bellicosity and his amatory sentiments arrested eighteenth-century commentators. This was a result of a mistranslation in Worm's edition of a Norse negation, which unfortunately made it appear as a simile with positive implications here, as well as in stanzas 14 and 18. In fact, the Norse *–at* suffix in the original (*vasat*) makes the sentences negative ("it was not as"). What was created was the picture of a warrior whose thoughts of war were imbued with romance, whereas, in the original,

the construction is used to set up a contrast between fighting on the battlefield and the comfort in domestic and erotic idyll. It was not before 1806, in William Herbert's *Select Icelandic Poetry* that this mistake was corrected by an English translator.

[8] Percy, following Ole Worm, refers to Harold I (called "Fairhair") of Norway (*Haraldr hárfagri*, c. 840–933). However, there is no legend mentioning Ragnar killing Harold, who would also have lived nearly a century too late for the two men to meet in battle. The appellation must refer to King Aurn, a Gaelic ruler of the Western Isles, whose name is mentioned in the original.

[9] One of the most striking images in Worm's translation was the phrase *ex concavis crateribus craniorum* ("the hollow cavity of the skulls"). These lines were annotated with the comment: *Sperabant heroes se in aula Othini bibituros ex craniis eorum quos occiderant* ("The heroes hoped they would drink in Odin's hall from the skulls of those they had killed"). This interpretation was based on the misconstruction of a *kenning*, i.e., a metaphorical compound phrase forming the basis of much skaldic poetry. The Old Norse *ór bjúgviðum haus*a [literally, "from the curved wood of heads"] is simply a substitution for drinking vessels made from

animal bone. This misunderstanding came to play an unwarranted role in the perception of Viking culture, as this line was often quoted.

[10] Odin's Valhalla. The poem remains somewhat of an aberration in respect to the tradition of brave heroes going to Valhalla, since only a few cases in the whole body of Old Norse literature point to a non-battle death as making the hero eligible for a place in Valhalla.

[11] In the original, Ragnar's concluding line, *læjandi skalk deyja*, literally translates as "laughing I shall die." These famous last words were often used to epitomize the idea of northern death-defiance. An illustration of this is S. Ferguson's translation in *Blackwood's Edinburgh Magazine* 33 (1833): 915, which emphasized Ragnar's celebration of death by introducing an emphatically jubilant interjection (with no basis in either Norse or Latin source texts): "E'en on my dying day,/ I'll laugh one other laughter yet — / Yet ere I pass away, Hurrah — hurrah — hurrah!"

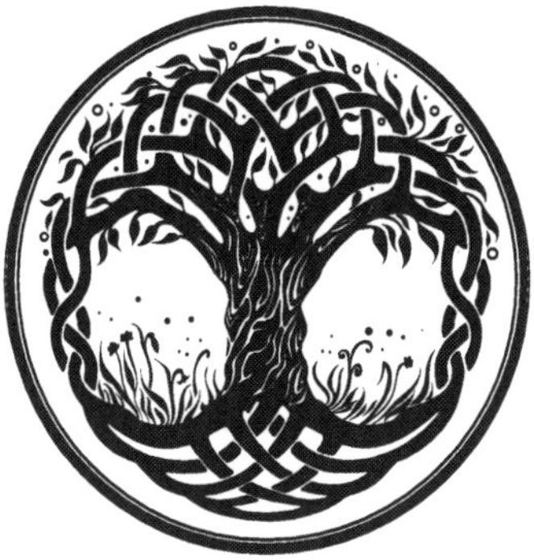

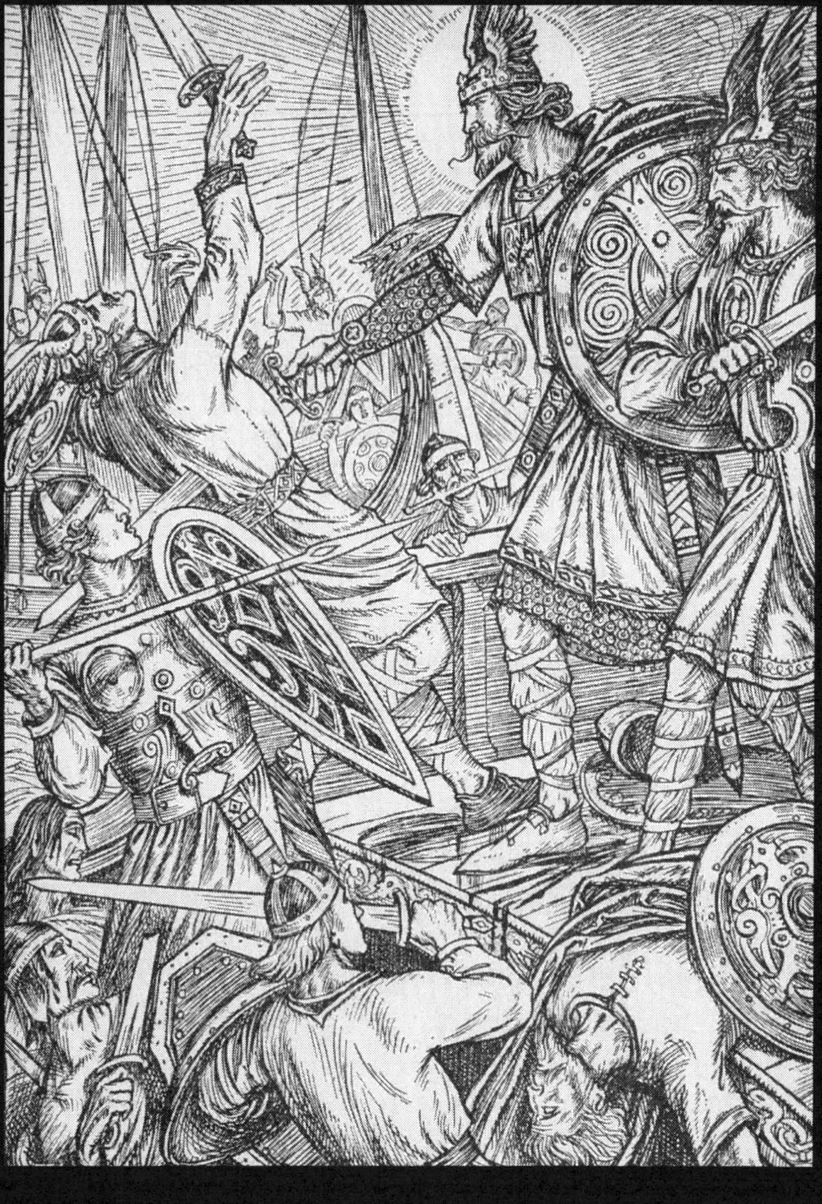

THE TALE OF RAGNAR'S SONS
14ᵀᴴ CENTURY A.D.

1.
KING RAGNAR

After the death of King Hring, his son Ragnar came to power in Sweden and Denmark. Then many kings came to the kingdom and seized land. And because he was a young man, they thought he would also be unfit for decision making or governing the country. There was a jarl in West Gautland who was called Herraud. He was a vassal of King Ragnar. He was the wisest man there was and a great warrior. He had a daughter, who was called Thora Hart-of-the-Town. She was the fairest of all women that the king had heard tell of.

The jarl, her father, had given her a baby snake for a present one morning. To begin with, she kept it in a box.

But in time, this snake got so big that it coiled right round the bower and bit its own tail. It grew so fierce then that no one dared come near the bower, except her servants and those who fed it, and it ate an ox a day. Folk were very scared, and they could see that it would do great harm, so big and fierce had it become. The jarl made this solemn vow at the *bragarfull*, the ceremony of the chief's cup, that he would give his daughter Thora in marriage to none but the man who could kill that snake, or who dared go and talk with her there in front of the snake.

And when King Ragnar hears this news, he goes to West Gautland. And when he had just a little way to go to the jarl's dwelling, he donned shaggy clothes: trousers and a cloak with sleeves and hood. These clothes were treated with sand and tar, and he took in his hand a great spear, and had a sword on his belt, and in this way he left his men and walked alone to the jarl's dwelling and Thora's bower. And as soon as the snake saw that a stranger had come, it reared up and blew poison at him. But he thrust his shield at it and went bravely toward it and pierced its heart with his spear. Then he drew his sword and cut off the serpent's head. And it turned out just as it says in the Saga of King Ragnar: he married Thora Hart-of-the-Town.

And afterward he went to war and liberated the whole kingdom. He had two sons with Thora, one called Eirek, the other Agnar. And when they were a few years old,

Thora takes sick and she died. After that, Ragnar married Aslaug, whom some call Randalin, the daughter of Sigurd Fafnir's Bane and Brynhild Budli's daughter. They had four sons. Ivar Boneless was the eldest, then Bjorn Ironside, then Hvitserk, then Sigurd. There was a mark is his eye, as if a snake lay around the pupil, and that's why he was called Sigurd Snake-in-Eye.

2.
THE DEATH OF RAGNAR'S ELDER SONS

Now when Ragnar's sons were fully grown, they went raiding far and wide. The brothers Eirek and Agnar were second in rank after Ragnar, and Ivar third with his younger brothers, and he was the leader because he was very clever. They conquered Zealand and Reidgotaland, Gotland, and Öland and all the smaller islands in the sea. Then Ivar set himself up at Hleidargard in Zealand with his younger brothers, but that went against the will of King Ragnar. His sons all went warring, because they didn't want to be any less famous than their father the king.

King Ragnar wasn't too pleased about this, that his sons had turned against him and taken his tributary lands against his will. He set up a man called Eystein Beli as king over Upper Sweden, and told him to hold the realm for him and guard it from his sons, if they laid claim to it.

One summer, when King Ragnar had gone east over the Baltic with his army, his sons Eirek and Agnar came to Sweden and brought their ships into Lake Mälaren. Then they sent word to King Eystein in Uppsala, telling him to come to them. And when they met, Eirek said that he wanted Eystein to govern Sweden under the brothers, and adds that he wants to marry Eystein's daughter Borghild, and says that then they'll be well able to hold the kingdom against King Ragnar. Eystein tells them that he wants to consult the Swedish chieftains, so with that they part. And when King Eystein raised this matter, the chieftains were all of one mind: to defend the land from Ragnar's sons. And they bring together now an overwhelming host, and King Eystein marches against Ragnar's sons. And when they clash, a great battle ensues and Lothbrok's sons are overwhelmed by superior numbers, and their troops fall in such numbers that hardly any were left standing. Then Agnar fell too, and Eirek was captured.

King Eystein offered peace to Eirek and as much of the wealth of Uppsala as he wanted in compensation for his brother Agnar and, along with that, he could have his daughter Borghild, just as he'd asked. Eirek didn't want any money, and he didn't want the king's daughter, and he says he doesn't want to live after such a defeat as he's just had. But this, he said, this is what he would accept: to choose for himself the day of his death. And since King Eystein couldn't get any settlement out of Eirek, he agreed to that.

Eirek asked them to catch him from below on spearpoints and so lift him up above all the slain. Then chanted Eirek:

"Don't care, cur, to hear you,
killer if you offer;
(Eystein, they say, slew Agnar)
I don't want your daughter.
To mourn me I've no mother;
make haste, hey!, impale me.
I'll die over host hoisted,
highest o'er the slaughter."

And before he was lifted up on the spears, he saw a man riding hard. Then he said:

"Send word to my slender
sweet stepmother, greet her:
(my forays east are ended)
say all my rings are hers.
Great will grow their anger

*when they get to know it,
when she brings her bounteous
boys news of my demise."*

Now it was done, just as he'd said: Eirek was raised up on the spear-points, and he died thus, up above the slain.

And when word of this reaches Aslaug in Zealand, she goes at once to see her sons and tells them the news. Bjorn and Hvitserk were playing tafl, and Sigurd was stood in front. Then said Aslaug:

*"I doubt, if they'd made it,
and you lot had fallen,
(with loved ones not living)
they'd let you go forgotten
—I say and make no secret—
six whole months sans vengeance,
if Eirek lived, and Agnar—
I who never bore them."*

Then Sigurd Snake-in-Eye answered:

*"In three weeks we'll be through with
(if that grieves you, mother)
(long the way that waits us)
war-readying of levies.*

Eystein's rule's soon over
—even if he offers
payments big and brazen—
if our blades prove true then.

Then said Bjorn Ironside:

"Heart will hold, heroic,
in a hawk-keen torso:
doughty, daring, though I
don't shout out about it,
nor snakes nor beady serpents
sit in my eyes spiralled.
Those men made me merry:
your stepsons I remember."

Then answered Hvitserk:

"Let's plan, before vowing,
how vengeance might be managed,
various vile torments
devise for Agnar's killer;
heave hulls onto billows,
hew ice aside, slice it.
Let's see whose sloop's scrambled,
schooners to sea, soonest."

Then Ivar Boneless said:

"Pluck you have in plenty
and pith as well with it:
let's trust too you're stubborn,
as tough heads are needed.
I'm borne before my fighters
forward though I'm boneless,
I have hands for vengeance,
though hardly strength in either."

After that, Ragnar's sons mustered an overwhelming army. And when they were ready, they went with a fleet to Sweden, while Queen Aslaug goes overland with fifteen hundred knights, and that host was well equipped. She wore armour herself and commanded the army, and they called her Randalin, and they meet up in Sweden and plunder and burn wherever they go.

King Eystein hears word of this and raises an army against them, with every man of fighting age who was in his realm. And when they met, a mighty battle ensued, and Lothbrok's sons had the victory, and King Eystein fell, and news of this battle spreads far and wide, and very famous it becomes.

Out campaigning, King Ragnar hears of it, and he's less than happy with his sons, as they'd taken revenge without waiting for him. And when he comes home to his realm, he says to Aslaug that he'll do deeds no less famous than his sons have done. "I've now won back almost all the lands that my forebears held, but not England. And that's why I've now had two *knorrs*[*] made at Lidum in Vestfold"—his kingdom reached all the way to Dovrefjell and Lindesnes.

Aslaug answered, "You could have had many longships[**] made for the price of these knorrs. And besides, you know that big ships are no good for going to England, with all the streams and shallows there, and this is not well thought out."

But all the same, King Ragnar goes west to England in these knorrs with five hundred men and both ships are wrecked in England, but Ragnar himself and all his crew came safely ashore. He takes now to harrying wherever he goes.

3.
THE FALL OF RAGNAR AND THE VENGEANCE OF HIS SONS

At that time, there was a king called Ella ruling over Northumbria in England. And when he learns that raiders have come to his kingdom, he musters a mighty

---

[*] Bulky cargo ships.

[**] Sleeker vessel favored as a warship.

force and marches against Ragnar with an overwhelming host, and hard and terrible battle ensues. King Ragnar was clad in the silken jacket Aslaug had given him at their parting. But as the defending army was so big that nothing could withstand them, so almost all his men were killed, but he himself charged four times through the ranks of King Ella, and iron just glanced off his silk shirt. Finally he was taken captive and put in a snake-pit, but the snakes wouldn't come near him. King Ella had seen during the day, as they fought, that iron didn't bite him, and now the snakes won't harm him. So he had him stripped of the clothes that he'd been wearing on the day, and at once snakes were hanging off him on all sides, and he left his life there with much courage.

And when the sons of King Ragnar hear this news, they head west to England and fight with King Ella. But since Ivar wouldn't fight, nor his men, and moreover the English army was immense, they were defeated and fled to their ships and home to Denmark, leaving it at that.

But Ivar stayed in England and went to see King Ella and asked to be compensated for his father. And because King Ella had seen that Ivar didn't want to fight alongside his brothers, he took this for a genuine offer of peace. Ivar asked the king to give him in compensation as much land as he could cover with the biggest old bull-hide he could find, because, he says, he can't very well go home in peace to his brothers if he doesn't get anything. This all seemed above board to Ella and they agree to these terms. Ivar now takes a fresh supple bull-skin and has it stretched out as thin as can be. And then he has the hide sliced into the finest string, and he then splits the flesh-side from the hair-side for himself. Then he has it pulled around a flat stretch of land and marked out foundations. He builds strong city walls, and that town is now called York. He makes alliances with all the people of the country and especially with the leaders, and eventually all the chiefs around pledged loyalty to him and his brothers.

Then he sends word to his brothers and says it's more likely they'll be able to avenge their father now if they come with an army to England. And when they hear that, they order out the army and make for England. And as soon as Ivar learns they're on their way, he goes to King Ella and says that he doesn't want to keep such news a secret, but he can't really fight against his own brothers; nevertheless he'll go and talk to them and try to make peace. The king agrees. Ivar goes to meet his brothers and incites them to avenge their father, and then goes back to King Ella and says that they're so savage and crazed with fury that they want to fight no matter what. As far as the king can see, Ivar is acting with the utmost faith. Now Ella goes against the brothers with his army.

But when they clash, a good many leaders leave the king and go over to Ivar. The king was outnumbered then, so that the greater part of his forces fell, while he himself was taken captive. Ivar and the brothers now recall how their father was tortured. They now had the eagle cut in Ella's back, then all his ribs severed from the backbone with a sword, in such a way that his lungs were pulled out there. As Sighvat says in the poem Knutsdrapa:

> "Ivar, he who
> held court at York,
> had eagle hacked
> in Ella's back."

After this battle, Ivar made himself king over that part of England, which his forbears had owned before him. He had two brothers born out of wedlock, one called Yngvar, the other Husto. They tortured King Edmund the Saint on Ivar's orders, and then he took his kingdom.

The sons of Lothbrok went raiding in many lands: England, Normandy, France, and out over Lombardy. But it's said the furthest they got was when they took the town of Luni. And one time they thought of going to Rome and taking that. And their warrings have become the most famous in all the northlands where Norse is spoken. And when they come back to their realm in Denmark, they shared out the lands between them. Bjorn Ironside got Uppsala and central Sweden and all the lands that belong to that, and it's told that Sigurd Snake-in-Eye had Zealand and Scania and Halland, and Oslo Fjord, and Agder as far as Lindesnes and a good portion of the Norwegian Uplands, while Hvitserk had Reidgotaland and Wendland.

Sigurd Snake-in-Eye married Blaeja, the daughter of King Ella. Their son was Knut, who was called Horda-Knut, who succeeded his father in Zealand, Scania, and Halland, but Oslo Fjord broke away from his rule. Gorm was his son. He was named after his foster father, the son of Knut the Foundling. He governed all the lands of Ragnar's sons while they were away at war. Gorm Knutsson was the biggest of men and the strongest and the most impressive in every respect, but he wasn't as wise as his forebears had been.

4.
OF KING GORM

Gorm took the kingship after his father. He married Thyri, who was called Denmark's Saviour, daughter of Klakk-Harald, who was king in Jutland. But when Harald died, Gorm took all of Harald's realm under his rule too. King Gorm went with his host over the whole of Jutland and abolished all the petty kings as far south as the River Schlei, and thus seized much of Wendland, and he fought great battles against the Saxons and became a mighty king. He had two sons. The eldest was called Knut, and the younger one Harald. Knut was the most handsome man ever seen. The king loved him above any other man, and so did all the people. He was called The Love of the Danes. Harald resembled his mother's kin and his mother loved him no less than Knut.

Ivar the Boneless was king in England for a long time. He had no children, because of the way he was: with no lust or love—but he wasn't short of cunning and cruelty. And he died of old age in England and was buried there. Then all Ragnar's sons were dead. After Ivar, Adalmund, the son of Saint Edmund's brother, took the kingship in England and converted large parts of it to Christianity. He took tribute from Northumbria, because that was heathen. His son, Adalbrigt, ruled after him. He was a good king and lived to an old age.

Toward the end of his time, a Danish army came to England, and the leaders of the army were Knut and Harald, the sons of King Gorm. They seized large parts of the kingdom in Northumbria, which Ivar had owned. King Adalbrigt marched against them and they fought north of Cleveland, and a great many Danes fell there. And a little later, the Danes went up to Scarborough and fought there and won. Then they marched south to York and the whole populous accepted their rule, and they had no fear. And one day, when the weather was hot, the men went bathing in the sea. And as the king's sons were also swimming between the ships, some men rushed down from the land and shot at them. Knut was mortally wounded with an arrow, and they took the body and carried it out to the ship. And when the English hear that, they gather their forces, so that the Danes can't get ashore, due to the Englishmen gathered there. So after that they go back home to Denmark.

King Gorm was in Jutland at the time. And when he heard these tidings, he collapsed and he died of grief at the same hour the following day. Then Harald, his son, ruled in Denmark. He was the first of his kin to take the faith and be baptized.

5.
THE FALL OF SIGURD HART

Sigurd Snake-in-Eye and Bjorn Ironside and Hvitserk had raided widely in France. Then Bjorn headed back home to his kingdom. After that, the Emperor Arnulf fought with the brothers, and a hundred thousand Danes and Norwegians fell there. There also fell Sigurd Snake-in-Eye, and Gudrod was the name of another king who fell there. He was the son of Olaf, the son of Hring, the son of Ingjald, the son of Ingi, the son of Hring, after whom Ringerike in Norway is known. Hring was the son of Dag and Thora Mother-of-Drengs.* They had nine sons, and the Dagling dynasty comes from them.

Helgi Hvassi, the Sharp, was the name of Gudrod's brother. He escaped from the battle with the standard of Sigurd Snake-in-Eye, and his sword and shield. He went home to Demark with his own forces and there found Aslaug, Sigurd's mother, and told her the tidings. Then Aslaug spoke a verse:

"Sad sit the corpse-stalkers,
slaverers after cadavers:
the slain-craver, raven—
what a shame!—forsaken
by namesake of Sigurd;
in vain now they're waiting.
Too soon from life Lord Odin
let such a hero go."

But because Horda-Knut was young, Helgi stayed with Aslaug for a long time as protector of the land. Sigurd and Blaeja had a daughter. She was Horda-Knut's twin. Aslaug

---

* *drengr* 'a gallant, brave fellow'.

gave her own name to her and brought her up then and fostered her. Afterward she married Helgi Hvassi. Their son was Sigurd Hart. Of all the men ever seen, he was the fairest, and the biggest, and the strongest. They were the same age, Gorm Knutsson and Sigurd Hart.

When Sigurd was twelve, he killed the berserk Hildibrand in a duel, and he single-handedly slew twelve men in that fight. After that Klakk-Harald gave him his daughter, who was called Ingibjorg. They had two children: Gudthorm and Ragnhild.

Then Sigurd learned that King Frodi, his father's brother, was dead. He went north to Norway and became king over Ringerike, his inheritance. There is a long story told of him, as he did all manner of mighty deeds.

But it's said of his passing, that he rode out hunting in the wilderness, as was his custom, and Haki Hadaberserk came at him with thirty fully armed men and they fought with him. Sigurd fell there, after first killing twelve men, but King Haki had lost his right hand and received three other wounds besides. Afterward Haki and his men rode to Ringerike, to Stein, where Sigurd's dwelling was, and took away Ragnhild his daughter, and his son Gudthorm, and plenty of goods too, and carried them off home with him to Hadeland. And soon after that, he had a great feast prepared and meant to celebrate his wedding, but it was put off because his wounds weren't healing. Ragnhild was fifteen years old then, and Gudthorm fourteen. Autumn passed, and Haki was laid up with his wounds till Yule.

At this time, King Halfdan the Black was staying at his estate in Hedmark. He sent Harek Gand with a hundred and twenty men, and they marched over the frozen Lake Mjøsa to Hadeland one night and came the next morning to King Haki's home and seized all the doors of the hall where the retainers were sleeping. And then they went to King Haki's bedroom and took Ragnhild and Gudthorm, her brother, and all the treasure that was there, and carry it off with them. They burned all the retainers in their hall and then left. But King Haki got up and got dressed and went after them for a while. But when he came to the ice, he turned down his sword-hilt to the ground and fell on the point and met his death there, and he's buried on the bank of the lake.

King Halfdan saw them coming over the ice with a covered wagon and guessed their mission had gone exactly as he wished. He had a message sent then to all the settlements and invited to all the important people in Hedmark to a big feast that very day. There he celebrated his wedding to Ragnhild, and they lived together for many years after. Their son was King Harald the Fine-Haired, who was first to become sole ruler over the whole of Norway.

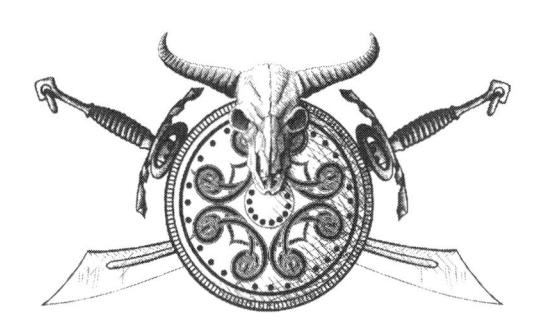

The Viking shieldmaiden Lagertha, wife of Ragnar Lothbrok

GESTA DANORUM (THE DANISH HISTORY)
BOOK NINE
14TH CENTURY A.D.

by Saxo Grammaticus

After Gotrik's death reigned his son OLAF; who, desirous to avenge his father, did not hesitate to involve his country in civil wars, putting patriotism after private inclination. When he perished, his body was put in a barrow, famous for the name of Olaf, which was built up close by Leire.

He was succeeded by HEMMING, of whom I have found no deed worthy of record, save that he made a sworn peace with Kaiser Ludwig; and yet, perhaps, envious antiquity hides many notable deeds of his time, albeit they were then famous.

After these men there came to the throne, backed by the Skanians and Zealanders, SIWARD, surnamed RING. He was the son, born long ago, of the chief of Norway who bore the same name, by Gotrik's daughter. Now Ring, cousin of Siward, and also a grandson of Gotrik, was master of Jutland. Thus the power of the single kingdom was divided; and, as though its two parts were contemptible for their smallness, foreigners began not only to despise but to attack it. These Siward assailed with greater hatred than he did his rival for the throne; and, preferring wars abroad to wars at home, he stubbornly defended his country against dangers for five years; for he chose to put up with a trouble at home that he might the more easily cure one that came from abroad. Wherefore Ring (desiring his) command, seized the opportunity, tried to transfer the whole sovereignty to himself, and did not hesitate to injure in his own land the man who was watching over it without; for he attacked the provinces in the possession of Siward, which was an ungrateful requital for the defence of their common country. Therefore, some of the Zealanders who were more zealous for Siward, in order to show him firmer loyalty in his absence, proclaimed his son Ragnar as king, when he was scarcely dragged out of his cradle. Not but what they knew he was too young to govern; yet they hoped that such a gage would serve to rouse their sluggish allies against Ring. But, when Ring heard that Siward had meantime returned from his expedition, he attacked the Zealanders with a large force, and proclaimed that they should perish by the sword if they did not surrender; but the Zealanders, who were bidden to choose between shame and peril, were so few that they distrusted their strength, and requested a truce to consider the matter. It was granted; but, since it did not seem open to them to seek the favor of Siward, nor honorable to embrace that of Ring, they wavered long in perplexity between fear and shame. In this plight even the old were at a loss for counsel; but Ragnar, who chanced to be present at the assembly, said: "The short bow shoots its shaft suddenly. Though it may seem the hardihood of a boy that I venture to forestall the speech of the elders, yet I pray you to pardon my errors, and be indulgent to my unripe words. Yet the counsellor of wisdom is not to be spurned, though he seem contemptible; for the teaching of profitable things should be drunk in with an open mind. Now it is shameful that we should be branded as deserters and runaways, but it is just as foolhardy to venture above our strength; and thus there is proved to be equal blame either way. We must, then, pretend to go over to the enemy, but, when a chance comes in our way, we must desert him betimes. It will thus be better to forestall the wrath of our foe by reigned obedience than, by refusing it, to give him a weapon wherewith to attack us yet more harshly; for if we decline the sway of the stronger, are we not simply turning his arms against our own throat? Intricate devices are often the best nurse of craft. You need cunning to trap a fox." By this sound counsel he dispelled the wavering of his countrymen, and strengthened the camp of the enemy to its own hurt.

The assembly, marvelling at the eloquence as much as at the wit of one so young, gladly embraced a proposal of such genius, which they thought excellent beyond his years. Nor were the old men ashamed to obey the bidding of a boy when they lacked counsel themselves; for, though it came from one of tender years, it was full, notwithstanding, of weighty and sound instruction. But they feared to expose their adviser to immediate peril, and sent him over to Norway to be brought up. Soon afterward, Siward joined battle with Ring and attacked him. He slew Ring, but himself received an incurable wound, of which he died a few days afterward.

He was succeeded on the throne by RAGNAR. At this time Fro (Frey?), the King of Sweden, after slaying Siward, the King of the Norwegians, put the wives of Siward's kinsfolk in bonds in a brothel, and delivered them to public outrage. When Ragnar heard of this, he went to Norway to avenge his grandfather. As he came, many of the matrons, who had either suffered insult to their persons or feared imminent peril to their chastity, hastened eagerly to his camp in male attire, declaring that they would prefer death to outrage. Nor did Ragnar, who was to punish this reproach upon the women, scorn to use against the author of the infamy the help of those whose shame he had come to avenge. Among them was Ladgerda, a skilled amazon, who, though a maiden, had the courage of a man, and fought in front among the bravest with her hair loose over her shoulders. All-marvelled at her matchless deeds, for her locks flying down her back betrayed that she was a woman.

Ragnar, when he had justly cut down the murderer of his grandfather, asked many questions of his fellow soldiers concerning the maiden whom he had seen so forward in the fray, and declared that he had gained the victory by the might of one woman. Learning that she was of noble birth among the barbarians, he steadfastly wooed her by means of messengers. She spurned his mission in her heart, but feigned compliance. Giving false answers, she made her panting wooer confident that he would gain his desires; but ordered that a bear and a dog should be set at the porch of her dwelling, thinking to guard her own room against all the ardor of a lover by means of the beasts that blocked the way. Ragnar, comforted by the good news, embarked, crossed the sea, and, telling his men to stop in Gaulardale, as the valley is called, went to the dwelling of the maiden alone. Here the beasts met him, and he thrust one through with a spear, and caught the other by the throat, wrung its neck, and choked it. Thus he had the maiden as the prize of the peril he had overcome. By this marriage he had two daughters, whose names have not come down to us, and a son Fridleif. Then he lived three years at peace.

The Jutlanders, a presumptuous race, thinking that because of his recent marriage he would never return, took the Skanians into alliance, and tried to attack the Zealanders, who preserved the most zealous and affectionate loyalty toward Ragnar. He, when he heard of it, equipped thirty ships, and, the winds favoring his voyage, crushed the Skanians, who ventured to fight, near the stead of Whiteby, and when the winter was over he fought successfully with the Jutlanders who dwelled near the Liim-fjord in that region. A third and a fourth time he conquered the Skanians and the Hallanders triumphantly.

Afterward, changing his love, and desiring Thora, the daughter of the King Herodd, to wife, Ragnar divorced himself from Ladgerda; for he thought ill of her trustworthiness, remembering that she had long ago set the most savage beasts to destroy him. Meantime Herodd, the King of the Swedes, happening to go and hunt in the woods, brought home some snakes, found by his escort, for his daughter to rear. She speedily obeyed the instructions of her father, and endured to rear a race of adders with her maiden hands. Moreover, she took care that they should daily have a whole ox-carcase to gorge upon, not knowing that she was privately feeding and keeping up a public nuisance. The vipers grew up, and scorched the country-side with their pestilential breath.

Whereupon the king, repenting of his sluggishness, proclaimed that whosoever removed the pest should have his daughter.

Many warriors were thereto attracted by courage as much as by desire; but all idly and perilously wasted their pains. Ragnar, learning from men who traveled to and fro how the matter stood, asked his nurse for a woolen mantle, and for some thigh-pieces that were very hairy, with which he could repel the snake-bites. He thought that he ought to use a dress stuffed with hair to protect himself, and also took one that was not unwieldy, that he might move nimbly. And when he had landed in Sweden, he deliberately plunged his body in water, while there was a frost falling, and, wetting his dress, to make it the less penetrable, he let the cold freeze it. Thus attired, he took leave of his companions, exhorted them to remain loyal to Fridleif, and went on to the palace alone. When he saw it, he tied his sword to his side, and lashed a spear to his right hand with a thong. As he went on, an enormous snake glided up and met him. Another, equally huge, crawled up, following in the trail of the first. They strove now to buffet the young man with the coils of their tails, and now to spit and belch their venom stubbornly upon him. Meantime the courtiers, betaking themselves to safer hiding, watched the struggle from afar like affrighted little girls. The king was stricken with equal fear, and fled, with a few followers, to a narrow shelter. But Ragnar, trusting in the hardness of his frozen dress, foiled the poisonous assaults not only with his arms, but with his attire, and, singlehanded, in unweariable combat, stood up against the two gaping creatures, who stubbornly poured forth their venom upon him. For their teeth he repelled with his shield, their poison with his dress. At last he cast his spear, and drove it against the bodies of the brutes, who were attacking him hard. He pierced both their hearts, and his battle ended in victory.

After Ragnar had thus triumphed the king scanned his dress closely, and saw that he was rough and hairy; but, above all, he laughed at the shaggy lower portion of his garb, and chiefly the uncouth aspect of his breeches; so that he gave him in jest the nickname of Lothbrok. Also he invited him to feast with his friends, to refresh him after his labors. Ragnar said that he would first go back to the witnesses whom he had left behind. He set out and brought them back, splendidly attired for the coming feast. At last, when the banquet was over, he received the prize that was appointed for the victory. By her he begot two nobly-gifted sons, Radbard and Dunwat. These also had brothers—Siward, Biorn, Agnar, and Iwar.

Meanwhile, the Jutes and Skanians were kindled with an unquenchable fire of sedition; they disallowed the title of Ragnar, and gave a certain Harald the sovereign power. Ragnar sent envoys to Norway, and besought friendly assistance against these men; and Ladgerda, whose early love still flowed deep and steadfast, hastily sailed off with her husband and her son. She brought herself to offer a hundred and twenty ships to the man who had once put her away. And he, thinking himself destitute of all resources, took to borrowing help from folk of every age, crowded the strong and the feeble all together, and was not ashamed to insert some old men and boys among the wedges of the strong. So he first tried to crush the power of the Skanians in the field, which in Latin is called Laneus (Woolly); here he had a hard fight with the rebels. Here, too, Iwar, who was in his seventh year, fought splendidly, and showed the strength of a man in the body of a boy. But Siward, while attacking the enemy face to face, fell forward upon the ground wounded. When his men saw this, it made them look round most anxiously for means of flight; and this brought low not only Siward, but almost the whole army on the side of Ragnar. But Ragnar by his manly deeds and exhortations comforted their amazed and sunken spirits, and, just when they were ready to be conquered, spurred them on to try and conquer.

Ladgerda, who had a matchless spirit though a delicate frame, covered by her splendid bravery the inclination of the soldiers to waver. For she made a sally about, and flew round to the rear of the enemy, taking them unawares, and thus turned the panic of her friends into the camp of the enemy. At last the lines of HARALD became slack, and HARALD himself was routed with a great slaughter of his men. LADGERDA, when she had gone home after the battle, murdered her husband. . . . in the night with a spearhead, which she had hid in her gown. Then she usurped the whole of his name and sovereignty; for this most presumptuous dame thought it pleasanter to rule without her husband than to share the throne with him.

Meantime, Siward was taken to a town in the neighborhood, and gave himself to be tended by the doctors, who were reduced to the depths of despair. But while the huge wound baffled all the remedies they applied, a certain man of amazing size was seen to approach the litter of the sick man, and promised that Siward should straightway rejoice and be whole, if he would consecrate unto him the souls of all whom he should overcome in battle. Nor did he conceal his name, but said that he was called Rostar. Now Siward, when he saw that a great benefit could be got at the cost of a little promise, eagerly acceded to this request. Then the old man suddenly, by the help of his hand, touched and banished the livid spot, and suddenly scarred the wound over.

At last he poured dust on his eyes and departed. Spots suddenly arose, and the dust, to the amaze of the beholders, seemed to become wonderfully like little snakes.

I should think that he who did this miracle wished to declare, by the manifest token of his eyes, that the young man was to be cruel in future, in order that the more visible part of his body might not lack some omen of his life that was to follow. When the old woman, who had the care of his draughts, saw him showing in his face signs of little snakes; she was seized with an extraordinary horror of the young man, and suddenly fell and swooned away. Hence it happened that Siward got the widespread name of Snake-Eye.

Meantime Thora, the bride of Ragnar, perished of a violent malady, which caused infinite trouble and distress to the husband, who dearly loved his wife. This distress, he thought, would be best dispelled by business, and he resolved to find solace in exercise and qualify his grief by toil. To banish his affliction and gain some comfort, he bent his thoughts to warfare, and decreed that every father of a family should devote to his service whichever of his children he thought most contemptible, or any slave of his who was lazy at his work or of doubtful fidelity. And albeit that this decree seemed little fitted for his purpose, he showed that the feeblest of the Danish race were better than the strongest men of other nations; and it did the young men great good, each of those chosen being eager to wipe off the reproach of indolence. Also he enacted that every piece of litigation should be referred to the judgment of twelve chosen elders, all ordinary methods of action being removed, the accuser being forbidden to charge, and the accused to defend. This law removed all chance of incurring litigation lightly. Thinking that there was thus sufficient provision made against false accusations by unscrupulous men, he lifted up his arms against Britain, and attacked and slew in battle its king, Hame, the father of Ella, who was a most noble youth. Then he killed the earls of Scotland and of Pictland, and of the isles that they call the Southern or Meridional (Sudr-eyar), and made his sons Siward and Radbard masters of the provinces, which were now without governors. He also deprived Norway of its chief by force, and commanded it to obey Fridleif, whom he also set over the Orkneys, from which he took their own earl.

Meantime, some of the Danes who were most stubborn in their hatred against Ragnar were obstinately bent on rebellion. They rallied to the side of Harald, once an exile, and tried to raise the fallen fortunes of the tyrant. By this hardihood they raised up against the king the most virulent blasts of civil war, and entangled him in domestic perils when he was free from foreign troubles. Ragnar, setting out to check them with a fleet of the Danes who lived in the isles, crushed the army of the rebels, drove Harald, the leader of the conquered army, a fugitive to Germany, and forced him to resign unbashfully an honor he had gained without scruple. Nor was he content simply to kill his prisoners: he preferred to torture them to death, so that those who could not be induced to forsake their disloyalty might not be so much as suffered to give up the ghost save under the most grievous punishment. Moreover, the estates of those who had deserted with Harald he distributed among those who were serving as his soldiers, thinking that the fathers would be worse punished by seeing the honor of their inheritance made over to the children whom they had rejected, while those whom they had loved better lost their patrimony. But even this did not sate his vengeance, and he further determined to attack Saxony, thinking it the refuge of his foes and the retreat of Harald. So, begging his sons to help him, he came on Karl, who happened then to be tarrying on those borders of his empire. Intercepting his sentries, he eluded the watch that was posted on guard. But while he thought that all the rest would therefore be easy and more open to his attacks, suddenly a woman who was a soothsayer, a kind of divine oracle or interpreter of the will of heaven, warned the king with a saving prophecy, and by her fortunate presage forestalled the mischief that impended, saying that the fleet of Siward had moored at the mouth of the river Seine. The emperor, heeding the warning, and understanding that the enemy was at hand, managed to engage with and stop the barbarians, who were thus pointed out to him. A battle was fought with Ragnar; but Karl did not succeed as happily in the field as he had got warning of the danger. And so that tireless conqueror of almost all Europe, who in his calm and complete career of victory had traveled over so great a portion of the world, now beheld his army, which had vanquished all these states and nations, turning its face from the field, and shattered by a handful from a single province.

Ragnar, after loading the Saxons with tribute, had sure tidings from Sweden of the death of Herodd, and also heard that his own sons, owing to the slander of Sorle, the king chosen in his stead, had been robbed of their inheritance. He besought the aid of the brothers Biorn, Fridleif, and Ragbard (for Ragnald, Hwitserk, and Erik, his sons by Swanloga, had not yet reached the age of bearing arms), and went to Sweden. Sorle met him with his army, and offered him the choice between a public conflict and a duel; and when Ragnar chose personal combat, he sent against him Starkad, a champion of approved daring, with his band of seven sons, to challenge and fight with him. Ragnar took his three sons to share the battle with him, engaged in the sight of both armies, and came out of the combat triumphant.

Biorn, having inflicted great slaughter on the foe without hurt to himself, gained from the strength of his sides, which were like iron, a perpetual name (Ironsides). This victory emboldened Ragnar to hope that he could overcome any peril, and he attacked and slew Sorle with the entire forces he was leading. He presented Biorn with the lordship of Sweden for his conspicuous bravery and service. Then for a little interval he rested from wars, and chanced to fall deeply in love with a certain woman. In order to find some means of approaching and winning her the more readily, he courted her father (Esbern) by showing him the most obliging and attentive kindness. He often invited him to banquets, and received him with lavish courtesy. When he came, he paid him the respect of rising, and when he sat, he honored him with a seat next to himself. He also often comforted him with gifts, and at times with the most kindly speech. The man saw that no merits of his own could be the cause of all this distinction, and casting over the matter every way in his mind, he perceived that the generosity of his monarch was caused by his love for his daughter, and that he colored this lustful purpose with the name of kindness. But, that he might balk the cleverness of the lover, however well calculated, he had the girl watched all the more carefully that he saw her beset by secret aims and obstinate methods. But Ragnar, who was comforted by the surest tidings of her consent, went to the farmhouse in which she was kept, and fancying that love must find out a way, repaired alone to a certain peasant in a neighboring lodging. In the morning he exchanged dress with the women, and went in female attire, and stood by his mistress as she was unwinding wool. Cunningly, to avoid betrayal, he set his hands to the work of a maiden, though they were little skilled in the art. In the night he embraced the maiden and gained his desire. When her time drew near, and the girl growing big, betrayed her outraged chastity, the father, not knowing to whom his daughter had given herself to be defiled, persisted in asking the girl herself who was the unknown seducer. She steadfastly affirmed that she had had no one to share her bed except her handmaid, and he made the affair over to the king to search into. He would not allow an innocent servant to be branded with an extraordinary charge, and was not ashamed to prove another's innocence by avowing his own guilt. By this generosity he partially removed the woman's reproach, and prevented an absurd report from being sown in the ears of the wicked. Also he added, that the son to be born of her was of his own line, and that he wished him to be named Ubbe. When this son had grown up somewhat, his wit, despite his tender years, equalled the discernment of manhood. For he took to loving his mother, since she had had converse with a noble bed, but cast off all respect for his father, because he had stooped to a union too lowly.

After this Ragnar prepared an expedition against the Hellespontines, and summoned an assembly of the Danes, promising that he would give the people most wholesome laws. He had enacted before that each father of a household should offer for service that one among his sons whom he esteemed least; but now he enacted that each should arm the son who was stoutest of hand or of most approved loyalty. Thereon, taking all the sons he had by Thora, in addition to Ubbe, he attacked, crushed in sundry campaigns, and subdued the Hellespont with its king Dia. At last he involved the same king in disaster after disaster, and slew him. Dia's sons, Dia and Daxo, who had before married the daughters of the Russian king, begged forces from their father-in-law, and rushed with most ardent courage to the work of avenging their father. But Ragnar, when he saw their boundless army, distrusted his own forces; and he put brazen horses on wheels that could be drawn easily, took them round on carriages that would turn, and ordered that they should be driven with the utmost force against the thickest ranks of the enemy. This device served so well to break the line of the foe, that the Danes' hope of conquest seemed to lie more in the engine than in the soldiers: for its insupportable weight overwhelmed whatever it struck. Thus one of the leaders was killed, while one made off in flight, and the whole army of the area of the Hellespont retreated. The Scythians, also, who were closely related by blood to Daxo on the mother's side, are said to have been crushed in the same disaster. Their province was made over to Hwitserk, and the king of the Russians, trusting little in his own strength, hastened to fly out of the reach of the terrible arms of Ragnar.

Now Ragnar had spent almost five years in sea-roving, and had quickly compelled all other nations to submit; but he found the Perms in open defiance of his sovereignty. He had just conquered them, but their loyalty was weak. When they heard that he had come they cast spells upon the sky, stirred up the clouds, and drove them into most furious storms. This for some time prevented the Danes from voyaging, and caused their supply of food to fail. Then, again, the storm suddenly abated, and now they were scorched by the most fervent and burning heat; nor was this plague any easier to bear than the great and violent cold had been. Thus the mischievous excess in both directions affected their bodies alternately, and injured them by an immoderate increase first of cold and then of heat. Moreover, dysentery killed most of them. So the mass of the Danes, being pent in by the dangerous state of the weather, perished of the bodily plague that arose on every side. And when Ragnar saw that he was hindered, not so much by a natural as by a factitious tempest, he held on his voyage as best he could, and got to the country of the Kurlanders and Sembs, who paid zealous honor to his might and majesty, as if he were the most revered of conquerors. This service enraged the king all the more against the arrogance of the men of Permland, and he attempted to avenge his slighted dignity by a sudden attack. Their king, whose name is not known, was struck with panic at such a sudden invasion of the enemy, and at the same time had no heart to join battle with them; and fled to Matul, the prince of Finmark. He, trusting in the great skill of his archers, harassed with impunity the army of Ragnar, which was wintering in Permland. For the Finns, who are wont to glide on slippery timbers (snowskates), scud along at whatever pace they will, and are considered to be able to approach or depart very quickly; for as soon as they have damaged the enemy they fly away as speedily as they approach, nor is the retreat they make quicker than their charge. Thus their vehicles and their bodies are so nimble that they acquire the utmost expertness both in advance and flight.

Ragnar was filled with amazement at the poorness of his fortunes when he saw that he, who had conquered Rome at its pinnacle of power, was dragged by an unarmed and uncouth race into the utmost peril. He, therefore, who had signally crushed the most glorious flower of the Roman soldiery, and the forces of a most great and serene captain, now yielded to a base mob with the poorest and slenderest equipment; and he whose lustre in war the might of the strongest race on earth had failed to tarnish, was now too weak to withstand the tiny band of a miserable tribe. Hence, with that force which had helped him bravely to defeat the most famous pomp in all the world and the weightiest weapon of military power, and to subdue in the field all that thunderous foot, horse, and encampment; with this he had now, stealthily and like a thief, to endure the attacks of a wretched and obscure populace; nor must he blush to stain by a treachery in the night that noble glory of his which had been won in the light of day, for he took to a secret ambuscade instead of open bravery. This affair was as profitable in its issue as it was unhandsome in the doing.

Ragnar was equally as well pleased at the flight of the Finns as he had been at that of Karl, and owned that he had found more strength in that defenseless people than in the best equipped soldiery; for he found the heaviest weapons of the Romans easier to bear than the light darts of this ragged tribe. Here, after killing the king of the Perms and routing the king of the Finns, Ragnar set an eternal memorial of his victory on the rocks, which bore the characters of his deeds on their face, and looked down upon them.

Meanwhile Ubbe was led by his grandfather, Esbern, to conceive an unholy desire for the throne; and, casting away all thought of the reverence due to his father, he claimed the emblem of royalty for his own head.

When Ragnar heard of his arrogance from Kelther and Thorkill, the earls of Sweden, he made a hasty voyage toward Gothland. Esbern, finding that these men were attached with a singular loyalty to the side of Ragnar, tried to bribe them to desert the king. But they did not swerve from their purpose, and replied that their will depended on that of Biorn, declaring that not a single Swede would dare to do what went against his pleasure. Esbern speedily made an attempt on Biorn himself, addressing him most courteously through his envoys. Biorn said that he would never lean more to treachery than to good faith, and judged that it would be a most abominable thing to prefer the favor of an infamous brother to the love of a most righteous father. The envoys themselves he punished with hanging, because they counseled him to so grievous a crime. The Swedes, moreover, slew the rest of the train of the envoys in the same way, as a punishment for their mischievous advice. So Esbern, thinking that his secret and stealthy maneuvers did not succeed fast enough, mustered his forces openly, and went publicly forth to war. But Iwar, the governor of Jutland, seeing no righteousness on either side of the impious conflict, avoided all unholy war by voluntary exile.

Ragnar attacked and slew Esbern in the bay that is called in Latin Viridis; he cut off the dead man's head and bade it be set upon the ship's prow, a dreadful sight for the seditious. But Ubbe took to flight, and again attacked his father, having revived the war in Zealand. Ubbe's ranks broke, and he was assailed single-handed from all sides; but he felled so many of the enemy's line that he was surrounded with a pile of the corpses of the foe as with a strong bulwark, and easily checked his assailants from approaching. At last he was overwhelmed by the thickening masses of the enemy, captured, and taken off to be laden with public fetters. By immense violence he disentangled his chains and cut them away. But when he tried to sunder and rend the bonds that were (then) put upon him, he could not in any ways escape his bars. But when Iwar heard that the rising in his country had been quelled by the punishment of the rebel, he went to Denmark. Ragnar received him with the greatest honor, because, while the unnatural war had raged its fiercest, he had behaved with the most entire filial respect.

Meanwhile Daxo long and vainly tried to overcome Hwitserk, who ruled over Sweden; but at last he enrapped him under pretence of making a peace, and attacked him. Hwitserk received him hospitably, but Daxo had prepared an army with weapons, who were to feign to be trading, ride into the city in carriages, and break with a night-attack into the house of their host. Hwitserk smote this band of robbers with such a slaughter that he was surrounded with a heap of his enemies' bodies, and could only be taken by letting down ladders from above. Twelve of his companions, who were captured at the same time by the enemy, were given leave to go back to their country; but they gave up their lives for their king, and chose to share the dangers of another rather than be quit of their own.

Daxo, moved with compassion at the beauty of Hwitserk, had not the heart to pluck the budding blossom of that noble nature, and offered him not only his life, but his daughter in marriage, with a dowry of half his kingdom; choosing rather to spare his comeliness than to punish his bravery. But the other, in the greatness of his soul, valued as nothing the life that he was given on sufferance, and spurned his safety as though it were some trivial benefit. Of his own will he embraced the sentence of doom, saying, that Ragnar would exact a milder vengeance for his son if he found that he had made his own choice in selecting the manner of his death. The enemy wondered at his rashness, and promised that he should die by the manner of death which he should choose for this punishment. This leave the young man accepted as a great kindness, and begged that he might be bound and burned with his friends. Daxo speedily complied with his prayers that craved for death, and by way of kindness granted him the end that he had chosen. When Ragnar heard of this, he began to grieve stubbornly even unto death, and not only put on the garb of mourning, but, in the exceeding sorrow of his soul, took to his bed and showed his grief by groaning. But his wife, who had more than a man's courage, chid his weakness, and put heart into him with her manful admonitions. Drawing his mind off from his woe, she bade him be zealous in the pursuit of war; declaring that it was better for so brave a father to avenge the bloodstained ashes of his son with weapons than with tears. She also told him not to whimper like a woman, and get as much disgrace by his tears as he had once earned glory by his valor. Upon these words Ragnar began to fear lest he should destroy his ancient name for courage by his womanish sorrow; so, shaking off his melancholy garb and putting away his signs of mourning, he revived his sleeping valor with hopes of speedy vengeance. Thus do the weak sometimes nerve the spirits of the strong. So he put his kingdom in charge of Iwar, and embraced with a father's love Ubbe, who was now restored to his ancient favor. Then he transported his fleet over to Russia, took Daxo, bound him in chains, and sent him away to be kept in Utgard.[*]

Ragnar showed on this occasion the most merciful moderation toward the slayer of his dearest son, since he sufficiently satisfied the vengeance that he desired, by the exile of the culprit rather than his death. This compassion shamed the Russians out of any further rage against such a king, who could not be driven even by the most grievous wrongs to inflict death upon his prisoners. Ragnar soon took Daxo back into favor, and restored him to his country, upon his promising that he would every year pay him his

---

[*] Utgard. Saxo, rationalising as usual, turns the mythical home of the giants into some terrestrial place in his vaguely-defined Eastern Europe.

tribute barefoot, like a suppliant, with twelve elders, also unshod. For he thought it better to punish a prisoner and a suppliant gently, than to draw the axe of bloodshed; better to punish that proud neck with constant slavery than to sever it once and for all. Then he went on and appointed his son Erik, surnamed Wind-hat, over Sweden. Here, while Fridleif and Siward were serving under him, he found that the Norwegians and the Scots had wrongfully conferred the title of king on two other men. So he first overthrew the usurper to the power of Norway, and let Biorn have the country for his own benefit.

Then he summoned Biorn and Erik, ravaged the Orkneys, landed at last on the territory of the Scots, and in a three-days' battle wearied out their king Murial, and slew him. But Ragnar's sons, Dunwat and Radbard, after fighting nobly, were slain by the enemy. So that the victory their father won was stained with their blood. He returned to Denmark, and found that his wife Swanloga had in the meantime died of disease. Straightway he sought medicine for his grief in loneliness, and patiently confined the grief of his sick soul within the walls of his house. But this bitter sorrow was driven out of him by the sudden arrival of Iwar, who had been expelled from the kingdom. For the Gauls had made him fly, and had wrongfully bestowed royal power on a certain Ella, the son of Hame. Ragnar took Iwar to guide him, since he was acquainted with the country, gave orders for a fleet, and approached the harbor called York. Here he disembarked his forces, and after a battle that lasted three days, he made Ella, who had trusted in the valor of the Gauls, desirous to fly. The affair cost much blood to the English and very little to the Danes. Here Ragnar completed a year of conquest, and then, summoning his sons to help him, he went to Ireland, slew its king Melbrik, besieged Dublin, which was filled with wealth of the barbarians, attacked it, and received its surrender. There he lay in camp for a year; and then, sailing through the midland sea, he made his way to the Hellespont. He won signal victories as he crossed all the intervening countries, and no ill-fortune anywhere checked his steady and prosperous advance.

Harald, meanwhile, with the adherence of certain Danes who were coldhearted servants in the army of Ragnar, disturbed his country with renewed sedition, and came forward claiming the title of king. He was met by the arms of Ragnar returning from the Hellespont; but being unsuccessful, and seeing that his resources of defense at home were exhausted, he went to ask help of Ludwig, who was then stationed at Mainz. But Ludwig, filled with the greatest zeal for promoting his religion, imposed a condition on the Barbarian, promising him help if he would agree to follow the worship of Christ. For he said there could be no agreement of hearts between those who embraced discordant creeds. Anyone, therefore, who asked for help, must first have a fellowship in religion. No men could be partners in great works who were separated by a different form of worship. This decision procured not only salvation for Ludwig's guest, but the praise of piety for Ludwig himself, who, as soon as Harald had gone to the holy font, accordingly strengthened him with Saxon auxiliaries. Trusting in these, Harald built a temple in the land of Sleswik with much care and cost, to be hallowed to God. Thus he borrowed a pattern of the most holy way from the worship of Rome. He unhallowed, pulled down the shrines that had been profaned by the error of misbelievers, outlawed the sacrificers, abolished the (heathen) priesthood, and was the first to introduce the religion of Christianity to his uncouth country. Rejecting the worship of demons, he was zealous for that of God. Lastly, he observed with the most scrupulous care whatever concerned the protection of religion. But he began with more piety than success. For Ragnar came up, outraged the holy rites he had brought in, outlawed the true faith, restored the false one to its old position, and bestowed on the ceremonies the same honor as before. As for Harald, he deserted and cast in his lot with sacrilege. For though he was a notable ensample by his introduction of religion, yet he was the first who was seen to neglect it, and this illustrious promoter of holiness proved a most infamous forsaker of the same.

Meanwhile, Ella betook himself to the Irish, and put to the sword or punished all those who were closely and loyally attached to Ragnar. Then Ragnar attacked him with his fleet, but, by the just visitation of the Omnipotent, was openly punished for disparaging religion. For when he had been taken and cast into prison, his guilty limbs were given to serpents to devour, and adders found ghastly substance in the fibers of his entrails. His liver was eaten away, and a snake, like a deadly executioner, beset his very heart. Then in a courageous voice he recounted all his deeds in order, and at the end of his recital added the following sentence: "If the porkers knew the punishment of the boar-pig, surely they would break into the sty and hasten to loose him from his affliction." At this saying, Ella conjectured that some of his sons were yet alive, and bade that the executioners should stop and the vipers be removed. The servants ran up to accomplish his bidding; but Ragnar was dead, and forestalled the order of the king. Surely we must say that this man had a double lot for his share? By one, he had a fleet unscathed, an empire well-inclined, and immense power as a rover; while the other inflicted on him the ruin of his fame, the slaughter of his soldiers, and a most bitter end. The executioner beheld him beset with poisonous beasts, and asps gorging on that heart that he had borne steadfast in the face of every peril. Thus a most glorious conqueror declined to the piteous lot of a prisoner; a lesson that no man should put too much trust in fortune.

Iwar heard of this disaster as he happened to be looking on at the games. Nevertheless, he kept an unmoved countenance, and in nowise broke down. Not only did he dissemble his grief and conceal the news of his father's death, but he did not even allow a clamor to arise, and forbade the panic-stricken people to leave the scene of the sports. Thus, loathe to interrupt the spectacle by the ceasing of the games, he neither clouded his countenance nor turned his eyes from public merriment to dwell upon his private sorrow; for he would not fall suddenly into the deepest melancholy from the height of festal joy, or seem to behave more like an afflicted son than a blithe captain.

But when Siward heard the same tidings, he loved his father more than he cared for his own pain, and in his distraction plunged deeply into his foot the spear he chanced to be holding, dead to all bodily troubles in his stony sadness. For he wished to hurt some part of his body severely, that he might the more patiently bear the wound in his soul. By this act he showed at once his bravery and his grief, and bore his lot like a son who was more afflicted and steadfast. But Biorn received the tidings of his father's death while he was playing at dice, and squeezed so violently the piece that he was grasping that he wrung the blood from his fingers and shed it on the table; whereon he said that assuredly the cast of fate was more fickle than that of the very die that he was throwing. When Ella heard this, he judged that his father's death had been borne with the toughest and most stubborn spirit by that son of the three who had paid no filial respect to his decease; and therefore he dreaded the bravery of Iwar most.

Iwar went toward England, and when he saw that his fleet was not strong enough to join battle with the enemy, he chose to be cunning rather than bold, and tried a shrewd trick on Ella, begging as a pledge of peace between them a strip of land as great as he could cover with a horse's hide. He gained his request, for the king supposed that it would cost little, and thought himself happy that so strong a foe begged for a little boon instead of a great one; supposing that a tiny skin would cover but a very little land. But Iwar cut the hide out and lengthened it into very slender thongs, thus enclosing a piece of ground large enough to build a city on. Then Ella came to repent of his lavishness, and tardily set to reckoning the size of the hide, measuring the little skin more narrowly now that it was cut up than when it was whole. For that which he had thought would encompass a little strip of ground, he saw lying wide over a great estate. Iwar brought into the city, when he founded it, supplies that would serve amply for a siege, wishing the defenses to be as good against scarcity as against an enemy.

Meantime, Siward and Biorn came up with a fleet of 400 ships, and with open challenge declared war against the king. This they did at the appointed time; and when they had captured him, they ordered the figure of an eagle to be cut in his back, rejoicing to crush their most ruthless foe by marking him with the cruellest of birds. Not satisfied with imprinting a wound on him, they salted the mangled flesh. Thus Ella was done to death, and Biorn and Siward went back to their own kingdoms.

Iwar governed England for two years. Meanwhile the Danes were stubborn in revolt, and made war, and delivered the sovereignty publicly to a certain SIWARD and to ERIK, both of the royal line. The sons of Ragnar, together with a fleet of 1,700 ships, attacked them at Sleswik, and destroyed them in a conflict that lasted six months. Barrows remain to tell the tale. The sound on which the war was conducted has gained equal glory by the death of Siward. And now the royal stock was almost extinguished, saving only the sons of Ragnar. Then, when Biorn and Erik had gone home, Iwar and Siward settled in Denmark, that they might curb the rebels with a stronger rein, setting Agnar to govern England. Agnar was stung because the English rejected him, and, with the help of Siward, chose, rather than foster the insolence of the province that despised him, to dispeople it and leave its fields, which were matted in decay, with none to till them. He covered the richest land of the island with the most hideous desolation, thinking it better to be lord of a wilderness than of a headstrong country. After this he wished to avenge Erik, who had been slain in Sweden by the malice of a certain Osten. But while he was narrowly bent on avenging another, he squandered his own blood on the foe; and while he was eagerly trying to punish the slaughter of his brother, sacrificed his own life to brotherly love.

Thus SIWARD, by the sovereign vote of the whole Danish assembly, received the empire of his father. But after the defeats he had inflicted everywhere he was satisfied with the honor he received at home, and liked better to be famous with the gown than with the sword. He ceased to be a man of camps, and changed from the fiercest of despots into the most punctual guardian of peace. He found as much honor in ease and leisure as he had used to think lay in many victories. Fortune so favored his change of pursuits, that no foe ever attacked him, nor he any foe. He died, and ERIK, who was a very young child, inherited his nature, rather than his realm or his tranquillity. For Erik, the brother of Harald, despising his exceedingly tender years, invaded the country with rebels, and seized the crown; nor was he ashamed to assail the lawful infant sovereign, and to assume an unrightful power. In thus bringing himself to despoil a feeble child of the kingdom he showed himself the more unworthy of it. Thus he stripped the other of his throne, but himself of all his virtues, and cast all manliness out of his heart, when he made war upon a cradle: for where covetousness and ambition flamed, love of kindred could find no place. But this brutality was requited by the wrath of a divine vengeance. For the war between this man and Gudorm, the son of Harald, ended suddenly with such slaughter that they were both slain, with numberless others; and the royal stock of the Danes, now worn out by the most terrible massacres, was reduced to the only son of the above Siward.

This man (Erik) won the fortune of a throne by losing his kindred; it was luckier for him to have his relations dead than alive. He forsook the example of all the rest, and hastened to tread in the steps of his grandfather; for he suddenly came out as a most zealous practitioner of roving. And would that he had not shown himself rashly to inherit the spirit of Ragnar, by his abolition of Christian worship! For he continually tortured all the most religious men, or stripped them of their property and banished them. But it were idle for me to blame the man's beginnings when I am to praise his end. For that life is more laudable of which the foul beginning is checked by a glorious close, than that which begins commendably but declines into faults and infamies. For Erik, upon the healthy admonitions of Ansgarius, laid aside the errors of his impious heart, and atoned for whatsoever he had done amiss in the insolence thereof; showing himself as strong in the observance of religion as he had been in slighting it. Thus he not only took a draught of more wholesome teaching with obedient mind, but wiped off early stains by his purity at the end. He had a son KANUTE by the daughter of Gudorm, who was also the granddaughter of Harald; and him he left to survive his death.

While this child remained in infancy a guardian was required for the pupil and for the realm. But inasmuch it seemed to most people either invidious or difficult to give the aid that this office needed, it was resolved that a man should be chosen by lot. For the wisest of the Danes, fearing much to make a choice by their own will in so lofty a matter, allowed more voice to external chance than to their own opinions, and entrusted the issue of the selection rather to luck than to sound counsel. The issue was that a certain Enni-gnup (Steep-brow), a man of the highest and most entire virtue, was forced to put his shoulder to this heavy burden; and when he entered on the administration that chalice had decreed, he oversaw, not only the early rearing of the king, but the affairs of the whole people. For which reason some who are little versed in our history give this man a central place in its annals. But when Kanute had passed through the period of boyhood, and had in time grown to be a man, he left those who had done him the service of bringing him up, and turned from an almost hopeless youth to the practice of unhoped-for virtue; being deplorable for this reason only, that he passed from life to death without the tokens of the Christian faith.

But soon the sovereignty passed to his son FRODE. This man's fortune, increased by arms and warfare, rose to such a height of prosperity that he brought back to the ancient yoke the provinces that had once revolted from the Danes, and bound them in their old obedience. He also came forward to be baptized with holy water in England, which had for some while past been versed in Christianity. But he desired that his personal salvation should overflow and become general, and begged that Denmark should be instructed in divinity by Agapete, who was then Pope of Rome. But he was cut off before his prayers attained this wish. His death befell before the arrival of the messengers from Rome: and indeed his intention was better than his fortune, and he won as great a reward in heaven for his intended piety as others are vouchsafed for their achievement.

His son GORM, who had the surname of "The Englishman," because he was born in England, gained the sovereignty in the island on his father's death; but his fortune, though it came soon, did not last long. He left England for Denmark to put it in order; but a long misfortune was the fruit of this short absence. For the English, who thought that their whole chance of freedom lay in his being away, planned an open revolt from the Danes, and in hot haste took heart to rebel. But the greater the hatred and contempt of England, the greater the loyal attachment of Denmark to the king. Thus while he stretched out his two hands to both provinces in his desire for sway, he gained one, but lost the lordship of the other irretrievably; for he never made any bold effort to regain it. So hard is it to keep a hold on very large empires.

After this man his son HARALD came to be king of Denmark; he is half-forgotten by posterity, and lacks all record for famous deeds, because he rather preserved than extended the possessions of the realm.

After this the throne was obtained by GORM, a man whose soul was ever hostile to religion, and who tried to efface all regard for Christ's worshippers, as though they were the most abominable of men. All those who shared this rule of life he harassed with divers kinds of injuries and incessantly pursued with whatever slanders he could. Also, in order to restore the old worship to the shrines, he razed to its lowest foundations, as though it were some unholy abode of impiety, a temple that religious men had founded in a stead in Sleswik; and those whom he did not visit with tortures he punished by the demolition of the holy chapel. Though this man was thought notable for his stature, his mind did not answer to his body; for he kept himself so well sated with power that he rejoiced more in saving than increasing his dignity, and thought it better to guard his own than to attack what belonged to others: caring more to look to what he had than to swell his havings.

This man was counseled by the elders to celebrate the rites of marriage, and he wooed Thyra, the daughter of Ethelred, the king of the English, for his wife. She surpassed other women in seriousness and shrewdness, and laid the condition on her suitor that she would not marry him till she had received Denmark as a dowry. This compact was made between them, and she was betrothed to Gorm. But on the first night that she went up on to the marriage-bed, she prayed her husband most earnestly that she should be allowed to go for three days free from intercourse with man. For she resolved to have no pleasure of love till she had learned by some omen in a vision that her marriage would be fruitful. Thus, under pretence of self-control, she deferred her experience of marriage, and veiled under a show of modesty her wish to learn about her issue. She put off lustful intercourse, inquiring, under the feint of chastity, into the fortune she would have in continuing her line. Some conjecture that she refused the pleasures of the nuptial couch in order to win her mate over to Christianity by her abstinence. But the youth, though he was most ardently bent on her love, yet chose to regard the continence of another more than his own desires, and thought it nobler to control the impulses of the night than to rebuff the prayers of his weeping mistress; for he thought that her beseechings, really coming from calculation, had to do with modesty. Thus it befell that he who should have done a husband's part made himself the guardian of her chastity so that the reproach of an infamous mind should not be his at the very beginning of his marriage; as though he had yielded more to the might of passion than to his own self-respect. Moreover that he might not seem to forestall by his lustful embraces the love that the maiden would not grant, he not only forbore to let their sides that were next one another touch, but even severed them by his drawn sword, and turned the bed into a divided shelter for his bride and himself. But he soon tasted in the joyous form of a dream the pleasure that he postponed from free loving kindness. For, when his spirit was steeped in slumber, he thought that two birds glided down from the privy parts of his wife, one larger than the other; that they poised their bodies aloft and soared swiftly to heaven, and, when a little time had elapsed, came back and sat on either of his hands. A second, and again a third time, when they had been refreshed by a short rest, they ventured forth to the air with outspread wings. At last the lesser of them came back without his fellow, and with wings smeared with blood. He was amazed with this imagination, and, being in a deep sleep, uttered a cry to betoken his astonishment, filling the whole house with an uproarious shout. When his servants questioned him, he related his vision; and Thyra, thinking that she would be blest with offspring, forbore her purpose to put off her marriage, eagerly relaxing the chastity for which she had so hotly prayed. Exchanging celibacy for love, she granted her husband full joy of herself, requiting his virtuous self-restraint with the fullness of permitted intercourse, and telling him that she would not have married him at all, had she not inferred from these images in the dream that he had related, the certainty of her being fruitful.

By a device as cunning as it was strange, Thyra's pretended modesty passed into an acknowledgment of her future offspring. Nor did fate disappoint her hopes. Soon she was the fortunate mother of Kanute and Harald. When these princes had attained man's estate, they put forth a fleet and quelled the reckless insolence of the Sclavs. Neither did they leave England free from an attack of the same kind. Ethelred was delighted with their spirit, and rejoiced at the violence his nephews offered him; accepting an abominable wrong as though it were the richest of benefits. For he saw far more merit in their bravery than in piety. Thus he thought it nobler to be attacked by foes than courted by cowards, and felt that he saw in their valiant promise a sample of their future manhood.

For he could not doubt that they would some day attack foreign realms, since they so boldly claimed those of their mother. He so much preferred their wrongdoing to their service, that he passed over his daughter, and bequeathed England in his will to these two, not scrupling to set the name of grandfather before that of father. Nor was he unwise; for he knew that it beseemed men to enjoy the sovereignty rather than women, and considered that he ought to separate the lot of his unwarlike daughter from that of her valiant sons. Hence Thyra saw her sons inheriting the goods of her father, not grudging to be disinherited herself. For she thought that the preference above herself was honorable to her, rather than insulting.

Kanute and Harald enriched themselves with great gains from sea-roving, and most confidently aspired to lay hands on Ireland. Dublin, which was considered the capital of the country, was beseiged. Its king went into a wood adjoining the city with a few very skilled archers, and with treacherous art surrounded Kanute (who was present with a great throng of soldiers witnessing the show of the games by night), and aimed a deadly arrow at him from afar. It struck the body of the king in front, and pierced him with a mortal wound. But Kanute feared that the enemy would greet his peril with an outburst of delight. He therefore wished his disaster to be kept dark; and summoning voice with his last breath, he ordered the games to be gone through without disturbance. By this device he made the Danes masters of Ireland ere he made his own death known to the Irish.

Who would not bewail the end of such a man, whose self-mastery served to give the victory to his soldiers, by reason of the wisdom that outlasted his life? For the safety of the Danes was most seriously endangered, and was nearly involved in the most deadly peril; yet because they obeyed the dying orders of their general they presently triumphed over those they feared.

Germ had now reached the extremity of his days, having been blind for many years, and had prolonged his old age to the utmost bounds of the human lot, being more anxious for the life and prosperity of his sons than for the few days he had to breathe. But so great was his love for his elder son that he swore that he would slay with his own hand whosoever first brought him news of his death. As it chanced, Thyra heard sure tidings that this son had perished. But when no man durst openly hint this to Germ, she fell back on her cunning to defend her, and revealed by her deeds the mischance which she durst not speak plainly out. For she took the royal robes off her husband and dressed him in filthy garments, bringing him other signs of grief also, to explain the cause of her mourning; for the ancients were wont to use such things in the performance of obsequies, bearing witness by their garb to the bitterness of their sorrow. Then said Germ: "Dost thou declare to me the death of Kanute?"* And Thyra said: "That is proclaimed by thy presage, not by mine." By this answer she made out her lord a dead man and herself a widow, and had to lament her husband as soon as her son. Thus, while she announced the fate of her son to her husband, she united them in death, and followed the obsequies of both with equal mourning; shedding the tears of a wife upon the one and of a mother upon the other; though at that moment she ought to have been cheered with comfort rather than crushed with disasters.

---

* Kanute. Here the vernacular is far finer. The old king notices "Denmark is drooping, dead must my son be!", puts on the signs of mourning, and dies

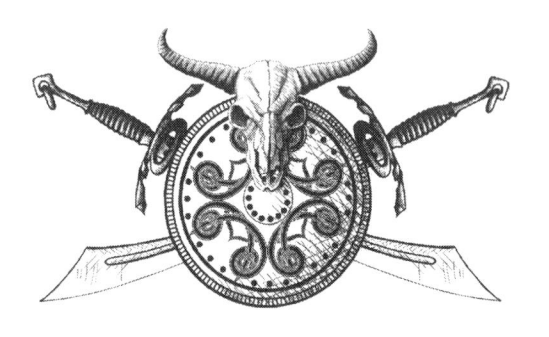